ALICE: GATEWAY TO EVIL

AL CE

GATEWAY TO EVIL

KERIE BELAS

INKWATER PRESS

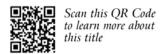 *Scan this QR Code to learn more about this title*

Belas, Kerie, author.
   Alice : gateway to evil / by Kerie Belas.
   pages cm
   LCCN 2015917297
   ISBN 978-1-62901-296-4 (paperback)
   ISBN 978-1-62901-297-1 (Kindle ebook)

   1. Demoniac possession--Fiction. 2. Exorcism--Fiction. 3. New York (N.Y.)--Fiction. 4. Horror fiction. 5. Thrillers (Fiction) I. Title.

   PS3602.E423A45 2015   813'.6
                      QBI15-600226

Publisher: Inkwater Press | www.inkwaterpress.com

Paperback ISBN-13 978-1-62901-296-4 | ISBN-10 1-62901-296-3
Kindle ISBN-13 978-1-62901-297-1 | ISBN-10 1-62901-297-1

Printed in the U.S.A.

3 5 7 9 10 8 6 4 2

TABLE OF CONTENTS

Chapter 1:   The Board 1

Chapter 2:   The Demon 21

Chapter 3:   Delilah 45

Chapter 4:   Father Seamus 67

Chapter 5:   The Archdiocese 79

Chapter 6:   The Exorcism 99

Chapter 7:   Deliverance 127

Chapter 8:   Linda 141

Chapter 9:   Not a Good Influence 151

Chapter 10: Back To The Girls 165

Chapter 11: The Answers 175

Chapter 12: Ivan The Terrible 183

Chapter 13: The Return 197

Chapter 14: Freedom .205

Chapter 15: An Unwanted Visitor 213

Chapter 16: The Epiphany 227

CHAPTER ONE

THE BOARD

It was a hot September night, and Alice O'Doyle was tired but could not go to sleep. She needed her backpack in order to do some homework, so she went downstairs to the inside porch to retrieve it. When she bent down, she noticed a Ouija board on a bookshelf.

Alice took the Ouija board to her room. She knew how to use the board. She lit two candles and placed her hand on the oracle.

Are there any spirits who would like to connect with me?

The board sat motionless.

Are there any spirits in the room?

The oracle went to yes.

Who are you?

The letters spelled out Brian. Alice asked Brian many questions. He was sixteen, and had died in a car accident.

Alice played until sunrise, then called and told Delilah, her best friend, about the Ouija board. Delilah said it was cool, and she would see her at school

Alice had breakfast with her Dad – Dr. Ryan O'Doyle.

Hey, Dad, I found a Ouija board last night; when did we get it?

I bought it for last year's Halloween party.

Can I have it?

Sure, just don't tell your mother.

Alice finished her breakfast and left for school.

Alice had a nice 1970 GTO, which she loved cruising around in. Delilah liked cruising around in her 2012 Porsche.

Alice and Delilah arrived at school at the same time.

Delilah, let's cut out this afternoon, go to my house?

Sure.

Alice's mom always took her Percodan with a glass of wine before lying down. Elizabeth O'Doyle was addicted to pills and alcohol.

Great, her mom was asleep when they arrived; they would go unnoticed.

Alice went upstairs to her room so she could retrieve her board.

We need to get some candles too.

Once they had everything they went downstairs.

Brian, can we speak to you?

The oracle moved to yes.

Brian, can you show yourself?

The board spelled out that Alice and Delilah would need to invite him. Alice and Delilah invited Brian to show himself. Neither knew what to expect.

They tried to reconnect with Brian, but the board went to Goodbye.

What happened, Alice?

I don't know, lost our connection I guess. Let's just listen to our iPhones for a while.

Maybe he is bored?

We're too hot to get bored over, Alice.

It really is way cool.

I wonder who moves the oracle?

Delilah, let's go upstairs and put the board in my room.

Brian, do you think I'm pretty?

Delilah!

The board spelled out S.L.U.T.

What's its problem, Alice?

I don't know?

Delilah went home at 4:00, the time she was to be home from school. Shirley Shipley asked her daughter if she was hungry.

Yeah, Mom, I would love some of that cold chicken from the fridge; I'll get some milk too.

Alice, was Delilah here? – I thought I heard her.

Yeah, she was over, she just went home.

Elizabeth looked at her clock – 4:10.

You get off from school early, Ally?

Yeah, Mom.

Grab your mom some Diet Coke, sweetie.

Alice knew the drill: Percodan and a Diet Coke to wash it down.

Guess I'll make supper.

Her mom might take too many pills, but she always was put together for her daughter.

3

Tacos, Mom, please!

Alright, Alice. So what's new and exciting at school?

Got my period in gym class.

I'm sorry, Ally, that's truly awful, especially for a six-teen-year-old.

No problem, I had my gear ready in my gym bag. Simon said hi to me.

Maybe the next time he may even ask you for a date.

Mom, I doubt it.

Why? You're a great catch for any guy. So I went to the doctor today, well, to see Kelly.

What did he prescribe for you today?

Stop talking to me in that tone. He prescribed me, if you need to know, Xanax. It's my nerves.

Mom, you stress out so much if Grandma's not here.

I know, baby.

Elizabeth's mom (Eileen McCary) was Elizabeth's security. She sheltered her from the world.

Okay, let's eat.

Are you going to eat, Mom?

No, not hungry.

You're never hungry. It's Mindy, isn't it?

What are you talking about?

Dad's Mindy, you know, his nurse?

Why do you worry so much about it?

I have my reasons.

Alice ate her supper, then headed off to do some homework. She had a book report on Sylvia Plath due. She loved her poetry so much.

She was doing her report when her night stand started to shake.

What is this, an earthquake in New York?

She checked on her mom – sound asleep. She went back to her room. It was very cold there, but no shaking of the night stand. *Must be traffic that caused it to shake.*

Dr. Ryan O'Doyle was late home from work again. Alice heard him come in, and went downstairs.

How's my baby?

Good, Dad, but my night stand was shaking.

Well, let's take a look.

The night stand was still when Ryan entered the room.

Well it's not now, maybe just traffic from outside.

Yeah, that's what I thought too.

Well, I'm heading for bed; Mom asleep?

Out like a light, so let's keep it quiet.

Morning came so early – back to the grind. Ryan was up early as always and off to work. Elizabeth came and took two Oxytocin to wake up, and Ritalin for her weight.

Morning, Ally.

Morning, Mom. Here's your morning cup of coffee, I am off for school. Where are my keys?

Alice looked and looked for her keys; she was going to be late.

Mom, where are my keys?

I don't know, Ally.

Shit, I'm going to be late.

Take my BMW, and I'll look around for them today.

Okay, I'm going to have to. I have a book report due, and I need to go.

Alice did not like the BMW. *It's a Mother car.*

Don't complain, it's a car.

Where are my keys, I wonder?

Time to focus on school. Alice read her book report on Sylvia Plath. It was well received.

That was a good report, Alice, a little morbid but good.

So Plath killed herself, Alice, said Mark, *too cool.*

It's not cool, Mark. Only an EMO like you would think that's cool.

Alice went to the school's store for lunch and bought herself a hot dog. She went to eat it at her locker with Delilah.

Do you know what is in those, Alice?

So good, replied Alice. *I don't eat salads all the time like you, girlfriend.*

I'm a babe, though.

You're in love with yourself. I brought the board to school – it's in my mom's car.

Your mom's car?

My keys went missing. Let's go to your house after school, Delilah.

Sure, no problem.

School went so slowly, but the bell finally rang. The girls left right away. When they got to Delilah's, no one was home.

Let's go down to the wine cellar.

Why the cellar, Di?

Well it's really dark.

Sounds good!

The girls set up and were ready to go.

Brian, can we talk to you?

The oracle went to yes.

Brian, am I pretty?

Delilah, please.

The board spelled out S.L.U.T.

Oh my God! Brian, that was uncalled for.

Delilah lost interest in the board after that. Neither girl was touching the oracle when it spelled out HATE!

What's up with this, Alice? What's its problem?

The candles blew out!

Oh shit, Alice and Delilah said together. Then both girls had a horrible feeling that someone was in there with them.

They screamed and ran in the dark to the door. It was locked, and they were truly frightened.

Alice, what's happening?

I don't know?

Delilah tried again to open the door – it flew open.

Alice, get rid of that board!

I will – it's too scary!

Both girls took it to the outside garbage.

Things did not seem so scary upstairs.

What was that all about, Alice?

I don't know?

Alice, did you see a shadow on the wall?

Yes, it was darker than the room.

Hey let's go check the Net and see what they say about Ouija boards.

They found out good or bad spirits come through. There were testimonials that demons could even be raised. Both girls agreed that it was a bad experience, and a bad ghost. They lied to themselves.

Alice went home and forgot about the board. She was listening to Courtney Love's song "Plump" on her iPhone upstairs. She thought she heard her mom calling and took off the earphones. Nothing. Well that was strange. She put back on her earphones. She loved Court; that's what she called her.

ALICE, YOU BITCH!!! came from the iPhone.

Alice ripped out her earphones, and ran to her mom's room.

Mom! Mom! You're not going to believe what happened. I was listening to my iPhone, and someone came through the phone and called me a bitch.

Elizabeth got out of bed slowly. *What are you talking about?*

I know it sounds weird but it happened!

Alice, it's that woman you listen to – Courtney Love.

No, it was not, it sounded like a growl. Alice was shaking.

Come here, love, crawl in bed with your mom. Alice was happy to do so.

You must have fallen asleep and had a nightmare.

Okay, Mom, I'm alright now.

Let's get supper, sweetie. Hamburgers, babe?

They had a great feast; even Mom ate.

Alice had a report due on Stalin.

How am I going to write this shit!

Just start, Alice, and use the Net.

She worked for hours on the report. When it was time to go to bed, she was afraid. *Okay it was just my mind playing tricks* – if only she didn't think she was lying to herself.

Alice went into a deep sleep. She had a nightmare where there was a man on fire with no eyes. She woke up in a sweat, and the room was ice cold. She turned on the light on the night stand and saw a dark hooded form. She screamed, and her dad came running into her room.

Daddy! God, that was scary.

What? What?

There was a man in a black robe and a hood!

Where?

In my room!

Come with me to get my gun.

We have a gun?

In the safe, in my room, come on.

Ryan and Alice went to the safe and got the gun. Funny, the security system did not go off. Ryan checked the house, but no one was there.

Alice slept in her parents' room. She was too scared to stay in her own. Sleep did not come easy for both her and her dad. In the morning her dad was at home.

No more Marilyn Manson for you, Alice.

What does Marilyn Manson have to do with anything, Dad?

Your nightmare with the black-robed man.

Oh please, Dad. Marilyn Manson is a very smart guy, he's just into his own thing.

Who is that woman that screams all the time?

That's Court.

Court? Who?

The one and only Courtney Love. Why are we talking about my music?

Well, I think this music seeps into your brain, Ally.

Dad, let's just leave it.

Ryan wanted to talk to Lizzy about Alice. Elizabeth had taken two Dilaudid and gone back to sleep.

Wake up, Lizzy!
What? What? I'm tired, just let me sleep.
Not this morning you don't. We need to talk about Alice!
That woke her up. *What about Alice?*
Did you not hear her scream?
When?
Last night! She thought there was a dark figure in her room.
It's that Manson guy; he gave her a nightmare.
What does she see in him, Lizzy?
Independent guy! I like him.
Lizzy, you really say the weirdest shit – independent guy!
He's harmless and I hear very smart.
My God, this house is filled with loons!

Alice came out of the bathroom and in the middle of her room were her car keys. *What's up with this? Whatever, I'm glad they're here.*

Too much strange shit was happening! *Well, my ride's back. Mom found my car keys.*
Where?
On the floor. You looked real hard, dear.
*I **did** look on my floor! This morning they just were there. Okay, Mom, coffee's made.*

Alice left for school in her GTO. She could not forget last night. *I'm sure I was not asleep, maybe I was. I've got to put it out of my mind.*

Delilah was on time for once. *Alice, I had the scariest dream last night.*
About what?
There was a man on fire, and he had no eyes.
Hey, I had that dream too.
What does it mean, Alice?

I don't know?

Maybe it has something to do with the board.

Delilah please believe me when I tell you this. I saw a black-hooded man floating around my room.

What?

It's true; I would not make up something like that.

Freaky. What did you do?

I screamed until my dad came.

It's the board, Alice!

Well, we got rid of it, okay?

Don't get touchy with me, Alice.

I'm sorry; I'm still freaked out.

Alice and Delilah went to class. There was no more talk about the board. Alice fell asleep in Language Arts.

Miss O'Doyle, please wake up.

I am sorry, Mrs. Ritchie.

That's fine. We are talking about Toni Morrison's Beloved.

I read it, Mrs. Ritchie.

Good girl.

I loved it.

Me too, Alice.

Alice loved reading books. Alice went to the school store after class to get some coffee.

Wow, I need this.

Alice looked at the cooler and saw a demonic face staring out at her.

What is that? screamed Alice.

The cashier asked what the problem was.

Your cooler has an evil face on it.

What face?

Why did she keep seeing things? Things she was sure

she saw. This time she told no one. School seemed to go by so slowly. After school she headed straight home. Mom was working out in the exercise room.

Hey, how fast is the treadmill going, Mom?

Alice, I need to lose ten pounds.

Ten pounds, are you crazy, Mom?

Oh, Alice, relax.

Alice went to her room, and in the middle of her floor was the Ouija board; she just stared at it.

What the hell is this? she said out loud. Now she was truly scared; it was the same board. The oracle started to spin, then stopped.

Alice! Alice!

What do you want?

Your soul, Alice.

Alice hit the floor.

When Alice woke up on the floor, she remembered the black figure. She went and threw up in the bathroom.

What is happening to me? She went back to bed, and shook for a long time. She must have fallen asleep, because when she woke up it was dark all over the house.

Mom must not have got up for dinner. She really needed to talk to her.

Mom, get up please! She was crying.

Ally, that you?

Yes, Mom, and I really need to talk.

Okay, what's wrong?

I saw that hooded figure in my room again. Don't say I was sleeping!

Alice you're starting to scare me.

No doubt, Mom, at least you believe me, unlike Dad; it's very scary.

Let's turn on some lights.

Right then Elizabeth saw the black hooded figure in the doorway! *Dear God, what is that thing?*

They both froze.

What is it, Mom?

I don't know?

The figure floated away. They could hear Emmitt the dog next. It was outside and it sounded like it was barking at the house. It scared Alice and Elizabeth.

What should we do?

Let's go downstairs; I'll get the gun.

The tension in the house was overwhelming.

Alice, stay close to me. They heard the garage door opening.

It's in the garage, Mom.

Stay back, Alice.

Her mom was very sober now. The door opened.

Stop right there or I'll fucking blow your face off.

What in hell is going on? Why no lights?

Oh God! It's you, Ryan!

What the hell! Are you high?

SHUT UP! We have had a scare like no other.

Ryan was very upset with Lizzy. *You don't point a gun at someone unless you mean to blow their head off.*

I'm so sorry, Ryan. I saw that black hooded figure, the same one Alice saw.

What a load of crap. You're both imagining things. Put the gun away, Lizzy.

Here, you take it, Ryan! Lock this gun up.

Okay then, can you two tell me what happened?
Alice and Elizabeth told their stories to Ryan. He was certain of one thing: they did see something. They were too scared to have made the story up.
Listen, you guys, I believe you saw something. What you saw makes no sense.
Well it was real enough, said Lizzy.
Okay, we have had a scare tonight; let's all settle down now.
Dad, can I sleep with you and Mom?
Okay, babe.
It was a long night for Alice. She knew what she had seen – a dark-robed figure. She was not seeing things; her mom saw it too. She had not seen her cat, Biggie Smalls, in a couple of days either. She would look for him in the morning. Morning could not come soon enough. She felt sick to her stomach.
Dad, you awake?
It's five o'clock in the morning. Okay, I'm getting up, babe.
Dad, I really did see a dark figure; so did Mom.
Okay, we will figure it out tonight.
Dad, can I stay home? I don't feel well.
No problem, kiddo; wake your Mom up. I'll get her some coffee.
Mom, here's your coffee.
What?
Your coffee, Mom!
Thank you, sweetie.
I'm staying home today, I don't feel well.
Okay, I will take care of you. Let me have a bath first.
I'm just going to stay in your room, Mom.
Alice and her mom made the best of their day. Alice

was very tired, and wanted her own bed. Safe enough, it was daytime.

Mom, I'm going to watch TV in my room.

Okay, sweetie. Alice still was not feeling well. She was tired and fell asleep watching TV, but was awakened by a growling voice.

GET UP, YOU BITCH!

She flew out of bed.

Who is that?

All of a sudden her cat was floating in mid-air. *What the fuck is happening here?* Then she passed out.

Alice did not know how long it took her to come to. She sat up and ran to the bathroom to throw up.

Alice, what's wrong; are you sick?

She threw up again.

Open the door.

I can't, Mom – it's locked.

No it's not, open the door.

She got up and opened the door.

It was open! But it wasn't open before. I'm sick, Mom.

Let's get you to bed.

Alice went to sleep in her mom's bed. That was the last day Alice was Alice.

When Alice woke up she arched her back all the way to her feet. Alice's mom stared incredulously, thinking Alice was high.

Alice, did you take any of my pills?

Then Alice soiled herself.

Elizabeth asked Alice if she was sick.

I AM SICK OF YOUR FUCKING MOUTH!

Ally, what's wrong with you?

ALICE DOESN'T LIVE HERE ANYMORE!
I'm calling your dad; you're very sick.
Nancy, please get Ryan; Alice is very sick.
He is in with Mrs. King.
Alice grabbed the phone out of her hand and swung it across her mom's face. The line went dead.
Hello, Lizzy? Lizzy?
She ran and got Dr. O'Doyle. Ryan ran to get his cell. He called on all phones – no answer.
I'm leaving – cancel all my appointments!
Ryan never sped, but he did today. When he got home he set off the alarm. *Shit, the security company was going to call. Lizzy? Alice? What's wrong?*
Ryan ran up the stairs rapidly. Alice was sitting cross-legged across her mother.
WELL, I SEE YOU'RE NOT OUT WITH YOUR WHORE.
Alice, you're sick. Come to me.
ALICE DOESN'T LIVE HERE ANYMORE, FAGGOT.
Let me help your mom, Alice.
LEAVE THE MAGGOT! SHE IS MINE.
Alice you're sick, and your mom is hurt!
ALICE DOESN'T LIVE HERE ANYMORE!
That's when she lunged towards her Dad.
Ryan tried to hold her back. She was too strong. She was on top of him. Then she saw his St. Michael's medallion.
IZGORILO.
That's when Ryan overpowered her.
STAY AWAY FROM ME, YOU CUNT.
Ryan ran to Lizzy's night stand and grabbed the

needle and morphine bottle. He knew Lizzy was mainlining it. He had an injection ready in minutes. He grabbed Alice by the shirt and injected. This stunned her enough for him to regain his strength. She stared at him with black eyes, filled with hate. Ryan held up his medal. Alice fell.

What in the name of the Lord was he seeing?

Ryan did not know who to call, so he called his associate, Kelly O'Dowd.

Nancy, put me through to Kelly right now.

He's with a patient.

It's Dr. O'Doyle. Get him for me.

Kelly, pick up the call. Kelly! Kelly! Come quick! Come here now.

Come quick where?

My house!

I have an office full of patients!

Come now!

Kelly O'Dowd knew he had to go.

Nancy, I'm leaving – cancel my patients.

What?

Kelly wanted to be there for his best friend, so he left. He tried Ryan's cell and all other phones. No answer.

What the hell is happening with Ryan? He was at Ryan's in twenty minutes. Ryan came to the door.

God, Kelly, thanks for coming.

What's wrong, Ryan?

Alice has gone mad and I'm frightened of her. I didn't want to call anybody but you.

What? Why?

Let's go upstairs.

Kelly saw Lizzy on the floor and Alice asleep.

Why did you not call 911? She needs medical care, Ryan.

I don't know? I gave Alice an injection of morphine.

Why, Ryan?

She attacked Lizzy, as you can see. I have checked her vitals, both of their vitals; they both are fine.

Kelly tried to arouse Lizzy.

Lizzy, Lizzy, wake up!

Lizzy moaned.

Come on, Lizzy, wake up!

Kelly, that you?

Thank God, thought Kelly.

Here, Lizzy, get on the bed.

Ryan and Kelly got Lizzy off the floor.

What happened? asked Ryan.

Alice went crazy, she hit me with the phone. She truly scares me, Ryan.

She's our daughter, Lizzy; we need to help her.

I know, I know.

Kelly and I will assess the situation when she wakes up. I injected her with your morphine.

Lizzy had nothing to say.

Where did you get the morphine?

We have bigger problems than that right now, Ryan.

Kelly, she is violent, said Ryan.

Well, all the more reason to get her medical care.

We are her medical care. She has two doctors here. I need to get some belts.

What for, Ryan?

To restrain her, Kelly.

Oh God, Ryan you can't mean it.

I do, Kelly.

Ryan grabbed two belts from his closet, restrained Alice's arms behind her back, and put a belt around her feet.

It was a long night for all of them. Lizzy did not want go to the E.R. She wanted to stay with her daughter – that's what a mother does. Alice was beginning to arouse. *WHAT HAVE YOU DONE TO ME, YOU COCK-SUCKERS?*

Alice, you're very sick.

UNSTRAP ME ,YOU ASSHOLE!

Kelly could only stare at her. *Alice? Alice? It's me, Kelly. WHAT DO YOU WANT, MAGGOT?*

Alice, you're very sick; let me help you. Alice just stared at him with black eyes.

She was truly frightening to look at.

God, what's wrong with her?

We need to get her to the hospital, Ryan, Kelly pleaded.

No, we will not have our daughter committed, Kelly. We want her with us, replied Lizzy.

What can we do then? Come on, guys, she's out of her mind.

I am going to give my daughter regulated shots of morphine.

That's a terrible plan, Ryan.

I agree with my husband, Kelly; she stays with us.

CHAPTER TWO

THE DEMON

K elly had to leave to get some rope.

Why am I doing this? I should call an ambulance.

He did it because he knew if she was treated at St. Michael's, the hospital would keep her in worse conditions. So he bought some rope.

Ryan had hired Kelly O'Dowd straight out of med school. He always treated him as an equal. *Whatever was happening with Alice? She was in a safe place, but were they?* Kelly brought the rope for Ryan and then left for the office.

They placed Alice in her bed and restrained her with rope. Ryan was giving her 5 mg of morphine every four hours.

Ryan, what is wrong with our daughter? I thought she got into some of my pills, Ryan. Then I remembered I had them in a lock box.

I don't honestly know what's wrong with our daughter, Lizzy. I only know I have to get more morphine.

Don't overdose her, Ryan!

I'm a doctor. I know how to administer medications. In theory it will work.

I am going to call Ken Darby – he is the best in the psychiatric field. He is not my favorite guy, but I'll call.

He's coming, Elizabeth.

Elizabeth was upset. She had had an affair with Ken to get back at Ryan for cheating on her, and lying to her. He would never admit his affair with Mindy. *Okay,* she thought, *Ryan has no idea about Ken. He was always at work with Mindy.* Elizabeth took pills to forget but she never could. The doorbell rang.

Hi, Ryan, long time. Ryan knew about Ken Darby; he was the last person he wanted to see, but it was for Alice.

Hi, Ken, it's Alice; like I told you, she is very sick.

Ryan was crying.

What's wrong with Alice, Ryan?

I think she is psychotic.

Why is she not at St Michael's?

I don't want to do that!

Okay, Ryan, I'll examine her. I'll do it for Lizzy and Alice – bring me to her?

Ryan brought Ken to Alice's room.

The first thing Ken saw was Alice tied up.

Why is she tied up! What in the name of hell are you doing, Ryan? You can't be serious.

She's violent. I have been giving her morphine.

Morphine is for pain, not psychosis.

I know but it was the only thing I had.

I won't even ask, Ryan.

Alice, can you hear me?

YES ,DOCTOR, I HEAR YOU! I KNOW WHO YOU ARE. YOUR WORK HAS NOT GONE UNNOTICED.

Untie her, Ryan!

No!

Lizzy had come to the doorway. Ken took one look at Elizabeth and was shocked.

What happened to you, Elizabeth?

Alice hit me with the phone.

Alice? Alice!

Leave her tied up, Ken, for me.

Alice, what's happened to you?

ALICE DOESN'T LIVE HERE ANYMORE!

Who are you then?

THE ONE WHO SHE SUMMONSED!

Alice?

I TOLD YOU, ALICE DOESN'T LIVE HERE ANYMORE!

Who are you then?

I AM A PIT DWELLER! YOU'RE IN LOVE WITH THE CUNT. WE HAVE BEEN WATCHING YOU. SINNERS LIKE YOU ARE ALWAYS NOTICED!

Alice, please listen to me; you're sick, said Dr. Darby.

I'M NOT SICK. I WILL STAY UNTIL THE MAGGOTS COME OUT OF HER EYES.

Ryan, I'm going to phone in some Seroquel – 100 milligrams. You can fill it at Walmart.

Sounds good, Ken.

Dr. Darby phoned it in. Ryan left to pick it up.

Elizabeth, I'm still in love with you; that's why I came.

It's over, Ken; please accept it, and help Alice.

I will never accept it's over, Elizabeth; I love you too much!

Ken grabbed Elizabeth by the arm and placed a kiss on her cheek. Elizabeth wanted to kiss him back, but needed to go see Alice.

Ryan came back with the Seroquel.

Alice, take this.

He tried to put the Seroquel with some water down Alice's throat. He could not do it; Alice was too strong.

We are going to have to get an injectable form. I'll try St. Michael's, but we will have to get a plan together after that.

Thank you, Ken, said Elizabeth.

Dr. Darby went to St. Michael's, where he had to be careful that no one saw him. He grabbed a bottle of injectable Seroquel, and headed back to Ryan and Elizabeth's house.

By the time he arrived Alice was awake.

She should still be asleep, said Ryan. *What did you bring?*

Seroquel.

Good, give her an injection.

Dr. Darby gave her 100 mg of Seroquel, but it had little effect. Her resistance to drugs was building.

Dr. Darby sedated her enough to slow her down and began to try to treat Alice.

Alice, you're awake?

DON'T CALL ME ALICE.

What should I call you?

PIT DWELLER.

Why pit dweller?

I COME FROM THE PIT OF SPITE AND HATE.

Do you mean to harm us?

YESSS!

Then we will have to keep you tied up.

DO YOU THINK SOME ROPE WILL STOP ME! ALICE IS IN THE PIT OF SPITE AND HATE. SO WILL YOU BE, KEN, IN TIME. MOMMY'S A SLUT, DADDY. SHE MISSED LOVER BOY.

What is she on about?

She's sick, Ryan; she doesn't know what she's saying.

Ken just looked at Elizabeth. Elizabeth turned away.

Ken, please help her, implored Elizabeth.

I don't know what to say to you all; Alice thinks she's a different person. She is showing signs of schizophrenia; she is at the right age.

Can we treat it?

Yes, but she will need an assessment at the hospital with my colleagues.

No hospital, Ken!

I would need a blood sample, Ryan.

I will get you a sample, but no hospital!

Elizabeth, please!

No! She stays with us.

Okay, but that's as far as I can treat her.

DO YOU KNOW DADDY IS WITH THAT WHORE MINDY, DR. DARBY? YOU ALWAYS GET HIS SEC-ONDS, Alice crackled loudly.

Ken looked at Ryan and Elizabeth.

YOU BOTH REEK OF HER.

How does she know all this? Have you told Alice about me? Ryan, Elizabeth?

No, of course not, they said.

How does she know these things?

We don't know, said Elizabeth.

Alice was starting to disturb Dr. Darby.

Alice remained in the state for hours.

You know, maybe she is suffering from Dissociative Identity Disorder.

You think so? said Ryan.

I don't know what to think; split personality is rare, and she doesn't have the traumatic background. I will see she is treated fairly at St. Michael's.

IZGORILO.

What does she keep saying?

Ken told Ryan he had spent a year in Croatia treating patients. *IZGORILO meant burn.*

Alice was trying to sit up.

Sit her up, Ryan, said Lizzy.

When I was young I saw a movie about demonic possession. That movie was a true story; I was so scared I had to sleep with my mother for months. What I don't understand is why Alice? Lizzy asked.

Please, Elizabeth, stop this. As a doctor and a friend, I'm asking you to please stop talking like that. She's in a state of psychosis.

The phone rang. Elizabeth was scared to answer it.

DON'T YOU WANT TO TALK TO THAT OLD BITCH?

Ryan answered the phone. *Hello, she's here, Eileen, hold on. Your mother wants to speak to you, Lizzy.*

Mom, Mom, is that you?

What's wrong, Elizabeth?

Mom, come to our house now!

Elizabeth, I just got off a very long flight from Ireland. Can it wait?

No, Mother; Alice is very sick.

Ally is sick? Why didn't you call me at Aunt Breda's? Mommy, please come!

I will be there in a zip; I need to catch a cab, sweetheart.

Eileen McCary was a devoted Catholic who went to Mass three times a week. She almost raised Ally. She was there in an hour.

Oh, Mom, I'm so glad you're home.

Elizabeth, what happened to your face?

Alice hit me with the phone.

Alice, or Ryan, hit you, bubble?

Alice! Why did she hit you?

She's very sick and very violent. Ken's here treating her so be nice.

Elizabeth, you know how I feel about Dr. Darby.

Please let it go, Mom!

Where's Alice?

Upstairs, we had to restrain her.

Restrain her? Why?

Like I said, she is violent.

Eileen took one look at Alice and was shocked beyond belief.

Why was not I called in Dublin?

It just started, Mom!

What's wrong with her?

We don't know.

QUIT STARING AT ME, YOU OLD COW!

Alice, watch your mouth, lassie.

ALICE DOESN'T LIVE HERE ANYMORE!

What are you talking about, lassie?

Alice just crackled, JA NEVOL NIKOGA.

Is she speaking in Croatian again, Ken?

Yes, it means I hate you.

Lord in heaven, she's like Paddy Fergus, replied Eileen.

Who is Paddy Fergus, Mom?

Paddy Fergus came from the old country. He was evil to the bone. He would have these fits in the Sheep's Head Pub. He would curse up a storm. He had the weirdest laugh. He told my ma that he was a devil. We believed him. He was a pig farmer. He used to say he liked to be alone with the swines. It was rumored that his house had pictures of hell in it.

Someone told us he was obsessed with these pictures. My da told me that he believed they were great art work; they were Hieronymus Bosch paintings. She is acting like him!

Well, he was probably very sick, Mrs. McCary.

Shut your gob, Ken, replied Eileen. *You're a smart ass!*

Mom! Stop it!

Eileen began to tell everybody all about Paddy Fergus's fits. Elizabeth was very frightened. Alice just listened in the beginning.

WOULD YOU LIKE TO KNOW WHERE YOUR PATRICK IS?

He's with God.

QUICK WITTED YOU ARE!

You sound like a Devil.

PADDY FERGUS SENDS HIS LUV. HE SAID HE LOVED PISSIN' IN YOUR POTATO FIELDS. DID SHE TELL YA BOUT YOUR BASTARD FATHER, PATRICK, ELIZABETH? HE WAS A WHORE! JUST LIKE YOU.

Elizabeth was speechless.

Only God and the Devil know that. You sure as shit are not God. Elizabeth, this is not Alice! I need to talk to Father Robert; he will know what to do.

Listen, Mrs. McCary, I know you despise me, but Alice needs to go to St. Michael's with me.

Over my dead body she does, you're not taking her anywhere. They will lock her up and throw away the key, that's what will happen.

No they won't, I give you my word on it.

Your words mean nothing, Ken.

Ryan and Ken had a beer.

You know she has to be treated. My colleagues should meet her too. St. Michael's is where your daughter needs to be. Not tied up at home, it's primitive.

Please, Ken, I didn't want you here, obviously. You're the best there is.

Well make you sure you watch the meds. Meantime 100 mg of Seroquel every four hours, no more than that.

Elizabeth and her mother were exhausted, but they needed to clean up Alice.

Elizabeth, let's give her a sponge bath.

Okay, Mom.

They cleaned her the best they could. Alice was still awake while they cleaned her.

GET YOUR FUCKING HANDS AWAY FROM ME!

Eileen just ignored Alice.

In the name of the Father, Son, and the Holy Spirit. Eileen and Elizabeth crossed themselves.

I WAS THERE WITH HIM WHEN THEY NAILED HIM TO A CROSS.

Eileen could not help herself, and she slapped Alice.

Mom, please stop that! It's not going to help.

I'm sorry, bubble. Look, bubble, I need to bring Father Robert here.

I know, Ma.

Tomorrow, Elizabeth, I'm staying here with Ally till I know for sure what's going on.

Ryan and Ken both sat down for a glass of rye whiskey.

Ken, I will always appreciate you for this.

Just be careful with the Seroquel.

I will, Ken; thanks for coming.

Ryan made coffee for Eileen and Lizzy, and Elizabeth came downstairs to talk to Ryan.

How about a shot for me, Ryan?

It's rye whiskey; you hate whiskey.

Not tonight I don't.

Help yourself, Lizzy.

Drinking, are we? said Eileen.

Ma, don't start.

Well you're on enough medication.

Let's not talk about it now, Ma.

Just let her have it.

Well I guess I'll join ya.

Eileen wasn't a drinker, but she had a few.

We can't just leave her upstairs tied up, you two, this is 2013.

I need to work out a plan. Ken will be over tomorrow, to check on her.

Eileen was very tired, but she knew sleep would not come to her. She went to Alice's room. *Alice?*

ALICE DOESN'T LIVE HERE ANYMORE ,YOU STUPID FUCKING BITCH.

What do you want with her?

HER SOUL, BITCH. SHE IS MINE UNTIL I TAKE HER TO THE PIT OF SPITE AND HATE.

No you're not, liar. I'm bringing some help for Alice. A priest to see her, how do you like that, you pig?

I WOULD LOVE IT. BRING FATHER SEAMUS TO SEE ME.

Who is Father Seamus?

HE IS IMPORTANT TO US.

Everyone stayed awake till morning.

In Dublin, Father Seamus was at his rectory preparing his Mass. He got up to open the he kitchen cupboard, and was swarmed by flies.

What in the name of Jesus!

There were flies everywhere. He didn't make the connection until much later. He got rid of most of the flies. That would have to do until Mr. McGee came in to clean that morning.

Father Seamus had no idea how the flies got there.

Mr. McGee came in at seven o'clock and was ready to clean.

We've got a fly problem, Mr. McGee.

No flies, Father.

You're joking me.

Church and rectory don't be having any flies, Father Seamus. It was clean when I left yesterday.

Well, it took me ages, replied Father Seamus.

Well, let me take a look.

They went into the rectory. Mr. McGee was shocked at all the dead flies.

You weren't joking me. Where did these little buggers come from?

I don't know, but I have spent a lot time on them. I have a Mass to prepare; please get rid of them.

Alright, alright, man, I'll take care of these buggers.

Father Seamus went back to his Mass.

Mass was full as always. Father Seamus was very loved and respected by his parish. After church a blind old lady approached him.

Are ya Father Seamus?

I am, Ma'am, what can I do for ya?

I wish you luck with the girl.

What?

You'll be a travelling man soon.

I'll be a what?

Like I said, good luck with the girl. My vision is gone but my third eye always sees clear.

Then she walked away.

I'll be a travelling man? Jesus, Mary, and Joseph, what a strange day it be.

Mr. McGee had the rectory cleaned when he came back.

Back in New York, Ryan, Elizabeth, and Eileen tried to form a plan.

Well, your man came here.

I want Father Robert, cried Eileen.

It couldn't hurt, said Elizabeth.

Father Robert could not make it till the next day. The day and night went by very slowly. They had Alice sedated, but it only stopped her acting out.

Thank you, Father, for coming so soon.

Anything for you, Mrs. McCary.

Like I said, it's my granddaughter, Father, she's very sick.

Why did you not call a doctor?

I am a doctor, said Ryan.

Oh I see, that's right; you told me your son-in-law was a doctor. Well I can pray with her.

She needs more than prayer, Father. Please come see her.

Alice was awake and sitting up when Father Robert went upstairs to her room. He was shocked when he saw Alice.

In the name of the Lord, why have you tied her up?

She will hurt you without the rope, said Elizabeth.

Did she do that to you, Elizabeth?

I'm afraid so, Father.

Alice stared at the priest malevolently. *WHAT DO YOU WANT, PRIEST?*

Alice, I'm here to help you.

SHE'S BEYOND YOUR HELP, DOGAN. YOU CAN'T SAVE HER.

How long has she been this way?

A couple of days now.

Alice?

ALICE DOESN'T LIVE HERE ANYMORE .

Who are you then? replied Father Robert.

I AM A PIT DWELLER.

A pit dweller?

ROBBER OF SOULS. SHE MADE A MISTAKE – NOW HER SOUL IS MINE!

Her soul belongs to Christ.

STILL DRINKING ON THE JOB, FATHER?

Father Robert did drink. Father Robert did not know what to say.

Who are you?

I TOLD YOU, I AM A PIT DWELLER. ALICE CALLED ME TO HER AND I CAME TO HER, SIMPLE

AS THAT. THE SLUT IS NEXT; LEGION WILL SEE TO IT.

What are you talking about?

THAT'S A SECRET! IN TIME ALL WILL BE REVEALED! YOU'RE A WEAK PRIEST, FATHER ROBERT. YOUR SOUL BELONGS WITH US.

My soul belongs to Christ!

YOUR SOUL BELONGS TO THE SWINES.

Father Robert did not like this conversation.

Please, let's take a break. I don't think she is sick. I hate to think the unthinkable.

What, Father Robert?

She sounds like she is possessed! Answer me honestly. Does your daughter dabble with the occult, or Satanism?

No, said Eileen and Elizabeth.

I want to look around her room.

It did not take him long to find the Ouija board in Alice's closet.

What is she doing with this?

We bought it for last year's Halloween party, said Ryan, *for a game.*

Why in God's name would you do that?

It's just a board game.

Ryan, these boards go back through the centuries. They are a gateway to evil. A board game is a gateway to evil.

Please, Father, she is sick.

Can you explain your daughter's sickness?

No, not yet, Father. Dr. Kenneth Darby has examined her. He is the best there is; he is best in the field of psychiatry.

Did he have answers, Ryan?

No but we did not want to take our daughter to St. Michael's

Kenneth Darby had a very busy day but he could not stop thinking of Alice. He would do anything for Elizabeth; she was the love of his life.

To think that arrogant Ryan O'Doyle had her. Everyone knew about Mindy and Ryan. Elizabeth did; that's why she was strung out on pills. Now Ken was dating Mindy to get back at Ryan.

I'm leaving the office now.

Yes, Dr. Darby.

Dr. Darby went to the med station. *800-mg bottle of Seroquel, Linda.*

Fill out the paperwork, Dr. Darby.

Sure, no problem, Linda.

Thank you, Dr. Darby. If I can be frank, Dr. Darby, you're awfully quiet today?

Long night, Linda.

Dr. Darby headed to the O'Doyle house.

Hi Ryan, Elizabeth, Mrs. McCary.

Hi yourself, slick, said Eileen sternly.

I am here for Alice, just like you are, Mrs. McCary.

She does not need your help.

Just then Father Robert came downstairs.

She is not sick like you think, Dr. Darby; please listen. Though it's good that you are trying to help.

We need a psychiatric opinion for the Archdiocese. Where did this girl learn to speak Croatian? She is speaking in a language she has no knowledge about. She is violent; she also reacts badly to religious material.

That does not make her need religious help. She needs to go to St. Michael's for treatment.

I don't agree, but I will not have this argument. I need to

35

get back to my rectory and contact the Archdiocese. The archbishop needs to be informed.

Dr. Darby needed to examine Alice. *I will go see Alice now, Father.*

Alice was awake and still looked violent.

WHAT DO YOU WANT, LOVER?

I want to talk to you, Alice.

SHE'S IN THE HERE WITH LEGION.

What is Legion then?

WE ARE MANY.

What does this have to do with Alice?

ALICE BROKE SOME RULES. USED HER HEART, NOT HER HEAD, WHICH ALLOWS ME TO BE HERE.

Father Robert spoke up.

Christ does not allow you to be here.

I WAS WITH HIM WHEN THEY NAILED HIM TO A CROSS.

Father Robert blessed some water and sprinkled it on Alice.

IZGORILO. YOU FUCKING CUNT. I WILL MAKE YOU PAY FOR THAT, PRIEST.

God is stronger, demon.

CALL ME A PIT DWELLER.

Alice crackled again, *WE ARE VERY STRONG, PRIEST.*

Like I said, God is stronger.

BRING ME FATHER SEAMUS.

Who is Father Seamus, demon?

OLD FRIEND. LEGION HAS A DEBT TO BE REPAID.

Back in Dublin, Father Seamus had just gone to bed

when he smelled something burning. He went to check his kitchen. It smelled like sulfur. He had smelled that smell when he was at Shawna McClellan's house for the Exorcism. He was afraid, he knew it was a sign.

St. Michael the Archangel, defend us in the day of battle.

Father Seamus's head began to throb; he tried to finish the prayer but could not.

St. Michael the Archangel, please help me.

The throbbing stopped. He knew what it was, and he began prayer. Father Seamus didn't stop for three hours.

Give me a sign, God.

He could see his breath in the rectory. That was his sign, he knew he would go into battle with darkness once again.

In New York, Ryan and Eileen were watching over Alice. Father Robert was just leaving, and so was Dr. Darby. Ryan was giving her the Seroquel. She had not slept in a long time. Ryan wondered why the Seroquel had no real effect on Alice. She kept asking for Father Seamus. They had no idea who she was talking about.

Alice, you need to eat and sleep, said Elizabeth.

I DON'T NEED IT, JUNKIE!

Why would she not eat or sleep?

WATER, I NEED WATER.

Father Robert came back into the room. He gave her water, but blessed it.

YOU'RE TESTING MY PATIENCE, PRIEST. She spit it out.

Give her regular water, Father, please; she needs to drink at least.

I COULD CARE LESS IF THE BITCH DIES!

Father Robert had to leave. He didn't want to.

Please, Ryan and Eileen, get some rest. I will stay up with her, said Elizabeth; *I have had sleep, you have not.*

Okay, but call if you need me, Elizabeth.

I will, Ryan.

Elizabeth realized she had taken little medication today. Just enough to stop the shakes. She was proud of herself. Alice needed her; she had to stay awake. She was mad as a hornet. She was also afraid of being alone with her daughter.

What do you want with Alice?

HELL IS HELL TO DEMONS TOO. SHE IS SO WARM, WE WILL STAY INSIDE OF HER.

I will bring your Father Seamus, if you tell me how!

HE IS ACROSS THE SEA, FIND HIM!

Just then the phone rang, and Elizabeth answered the phone.

Elizabeth, I met a Father Seamus in Ireland.

I asked Alice, Mom, where he was; she said he is across the sea.

I think it's him. Many people say he performed an Exorcism back some years.

Can you contact him through Breda?

I'll try at around three a.m. I should be able to reach her.

Eileen waited till three o'clock to call Breda. It took her awhile to get through.

Breda, that you?

Ya, Eileen, it's me. Just a little winded, was out and about in me garden.

Breda, I need a favor.

Anything, luv.

Alice is very sick.

What?

Breda, she keeps asking for Father Seamus. I only know one – the priest at your church.

Our Father Seamus?

Yes, please, Breda, it's urgent.

I'll call him at the rectory for ya, Eileen. What should I say?

Tell him he can call night or day. Tell him the Devil has come to our door!

Jesus, Mary, and Joseph. What are ya on about?

Tell him and see what he has to say.

Father Seamus had gone a walk. He had just got back to the rectory when the phone began to ring.

Father Seamus here.

Father Seamus, it's Breda McKinney from church.

How you doing today, Breda, luv?

Not too good, my sister, the one you met, wants you to call her. She told me you could call night and day.

What about, luv?

She said the Devil has come to her door, Father Seamus.

Father Seamus was speechless; he did not know what to think.

Give me her number.

Yes, Father, I have it right here.

Father Seamus knew what it was about. The girl across the sea. He breathed deep, and dialed the number.

Hello, is Eileen there by any chance?

Speaking, is this Father Seamus?

Yes, we met in Dublin; right, you're from the States.

Yes that's right, right it is, Father Seamus.

What can I do for ya, Eileen?

I think I need your help.

Why's that?

It's my granddaughter, Father, the Devil's in her, Father!

Why would you say that?

Believe me when I say the Devil's got her. Breda said you have performed Exorcisms.

Father Seamus asked why the Archdiocese there was not contacted.

Father Robert is going to. Alice, my granddaughter, keeps asking for a Father Seamus.

Could be any Father Seamus?

She said you lived across the sea.

Eileen, when did this start?

Couple days now. Father Seamus, never in all my life have I seen anything like it. Except for an old man from back home in Ireland.

Give me Father Robert's number, please, Eileen.

Sure thing, Father.

Father Robert could not sleep. He had never been around anybody who was possessed. He had met some bad people in his time, but nothing like Alice. *Why in God's name did they buy the board? You can get them at the toy store, that's why.* He should not hold anger against the family; they were just ignorant. The phone rang.

Father Robert speaking.

Hello, Father Robert, this is Father Seamus; is it too late for a call?

No, I wasn't asleep.

What is happening, Father Robert?

I don't really know for sure, but it looks like possession.

Why? Well I don't know all the criteria set out in the Roman Ritual. She speaks Croatian, a language she never learned. She is violent. Also she is very violent when it comes to religious objects, or the mention of St. Michael.

Interesting.

Did you know this girl before this happened?

Yes, her grandmother took her to Sunday school when she was young.

Please talk to your Archbishop, Father Robert, and call me when you have talked to him.

Thank you, Father Seamus; I'll see what I can do.

It took a while for the information to sink in. Surely they must have a Exorcist in the States that was available, who could perform the Ritual. Then he remembered the flies in the rectory, and the coldness in the rectory. He had asked God for a sign, and he received them.

The States, he had never been across the pond.

Well I am sure there is an Exorcist in the States who could perform the Ritual. He tried to put it out of his mind, but could not.

Father Robert gave the morning mass to his parish. There was no time to chat with his fellow parishioners. He needed to get back to see Alice.

He had placed a call in to the Archdiocese, and he was still waiting for the office to get back to him.

When Father Robert arrived at Alice's house, everybody looked shell-shocked.

Ryan greeted him at the door.

Hello, Ryan, how is she?

The same. She refuses everything but water.

Is she still tied up?

Yes, Father, we are trying to make her as comfortable as possible.

Good. Well, let's go see her.

Alice was the same. She had not slept; that was obvious.

Alice?

WHY DO YOU KEEP CALLING ME THAT WRETCHED NAME, PRIEST?

Well what is your name?

PIT DWELLER.

No I mean what is your name, demon?

WOULDN'T YOU LIKE TO KNOW!

Give me your name, demon!

IT IS FORBIDDEN.

I talked to a Father Seamus; he lives in Ireland, doesn't he?

HE LIVES IN THE LAND OF POTATOES, *Alice crackled.*

That's Ireland, isn't it?

THAT'S CORRECT, PRIEST.

Why do you want him specifically?

HE HAS A DEBT WITH LEGION.

You are Legion?

I HAVE MY OWN NAME, BUT I AM WITH LEGION.

Dr. Darby came by to see Alice.

How are you today, Alice?

WHO IS ALICE?

You are Alice.

I AM PIT DWELLER!

Okay, we can call you that, Pit Dweller. Do you know who Alice is?

SHE'S THE MAGGOT WHO SUMMONSED ME.

HOW IS IT FOR YOU TO BE SO CLOSE TO YOUR ELIZABETH?

Fine, she's a great person.

SHE WAS YOUR LOVER!

That's correct, Alice. How do you know this information?

I KNOW ALL YOUR FUCKING SINS!

CHAPTER THREE

DELILAH

Where was Alice? She had called her everyday on all phones. *Well, I will just have to go to her house today,* said Delilah.

Marko Bostic was the hottest guy in school. Delilah was in love with him.

Marko was going into the school store.

Well, time to make my move.

Hi Marko.

Hi Delilah. How's the Porsche?

Hot and fast!

Well, I like hot and fast.

Marko, do you want a ride in it?

Sure, as long as I can drive it.

Sure, no problem.

Okay, today after school, Delilah.

ALICE: GATEWAY TO HELL

Sorry, not today, you know my best friend Alice?
Sure.
She's gone M.I.A., so I really need to check on her! How about tomorrow, Marko?
Sure, I'll see you tomorrow.
Sounds great, Marko.

The day was way too long but exciting. After her last class, Delilah went to Alice's house. She rang the doorbell, but it took a while before anybody answered. Elizabeth came to the door.

Hi, Mrs. O'Doyle, is Alice here?
She's been sick, Delilah.
Well, can I go to see her?
She is too sick.
I won't be long!
No, Delilah, not today.
Can you please have her call me?
Delilah, is that you?
Yes, Alice, it's me.
HAVE YOU GOT A DATE WITH MARKO?
How did you know?
I SEE EVERYTHING, SLUT!
What did you say?
I CALLED YOU A SLUT!
She's sick, Delilah; like I said, it's better if you leave.
I'm leaving!

Delilah was pissed. What kind of sickness causes a person to call their best friend a slut? *She's just jealous that he chose me. How did she know?* How strange, too strange! She was scared now. *What kind of sickness comes with being psychic?* Delilah was not mad anymore; she didn't know what to think.

Delilah had a very scary dream about Alice. She dreamed she saw Alice in a pit of fire; it didn't even look like Alice anymore. She was standing by the man that was on fire with no eyes. When she woke up, she turned on the light – she was scared out her mind. She got her iPhone and listened to music. She started to get tired listening to the music and began to doze off when she heard *YOU'RE NEXT, BITCH!* It was Alice's voice. She threw off her earphones; Delilah was truly terrified. *That was Alice I heard on the earphones!* She had been listening to Nine Inch Nails' "Head Like a Hole." *I know what I heard, but how?*

She wanted to call Alice. Her cell rang twice and a voice came through the phone. *ARE YOU SEEING THAT LITTLE CUNT MARKO?* Delilah hung up!

What is wrong with Alice? She was going to find out.

Delilah called Alice's mother.

After three rings she answered. *Hello.*

What is your daughter's problem?

What are you talking about, Delilah?

I just called her and she said something vile!

Alice is asleep now, I have her cell phone.

What, but I just talked to her on her cell!

You couldn't have, Delilah. I'm in the middle of something so I will have to let you go.

Delilah was truly bewildered. *I know what I heard. What is going on at the O'Doyle house?* She had to find out.

Delilah had a hard time getting to sleep and had more nightmares about Alice. This time she was sitting on the roof of her Porsche. She had red eyes, and the Porsche was about to hit Marko. She sat up in bed, and turned on the lights.

Why am I having these nightmares about Alice?

She was truly frightened.

Delilah must have fallen back asleep, because she woke up late. *Shit! Shit! Shit! I have to sleep in on the day of my date with Marko!* She wore her black leggings with an Iron Maiden shirt. When she went to get in her car, there were three giant scratches! *What in the name of God happened? My car is ruined. I have to get to school, or I will be late again.*

Delilah kept a lookout for Marko, and she started to panic! *Where is he – we were to meet up at the school store at lunch time.* He was a no show.

After school he wasn't there either. Delilah waited an hour for him, but he never showed up.

Delilah drove home with a heavy heart. First her car, now Marko standing her up. It was a very bad day. She pulled into the driveway. Her dad was going to freak out over the car; it was her sweet sixteen present.

Trip Shipley was home when she came home.

Daddy, come check out the car.

Why, what's wrong?

Someone put three big scratches on the hood of my car.

What?

Please come see, Daddy!

Delilah started to cry. The day was all too much for her.

Trip Shipley owned a Porsche dealership. *Let's take a look, honey. Oh yeah, those are bad!*

What am I going to do?

Well, insurance will cover it. I'll get into the shop; you'll have to drive a rental till then.

Delilah was relieved; that one was less thing to be sad about.

Cheer up, baby; we'll get it fixed.

It's not just that, Dad. Alice has gone crazy, and the hottest guy in school stood me up.

Alice? What's up with Alice, honey?

I don't really know. Her mom said she is sick, but she doesn't act sick! She is mean. She called me a slut from her room. Then she phoned last night and she said disgusting things to me. I called her mom and she said she was sleeping.

That's strange; I'll call Ryan and see what's going on!

Trip called Ryan.

Dr. O'Doyle speaking.

Hey, Ryan, it's Trip Shipley calling.

Hi, Trip. Ryan sounded very tired.

Well, I was calling to see how Alice was doing.

Not very good, Trip; she is very sick.

Why did she call Delilah a slut yesterday?

I was not aware of that.

Yeah, Delilah came to check on her at the house.

Well, Trip, we're great friends, you are owed an explanation. Alice is sick, sick!

Like in the head, Ryan?

I'm afraid so.

Well, Ryan, I am truly sorry to hear that.

Thanks, Trip, sorry about yesterday.

Delilah, we need to talk, I don't know how to explain this to you. Alice isn't sick with some kind of flu, she is mentally sick.

What? Alice? Delilah started to cry. *I understand, Dad, but Alice is always so put together.*

Well she isn't right, honey, so give them their space.

Delilah went to her room and cried. Her life was falling apart. *Oh Alice, what can I do to help you?* Delilah fell asleep crying. She had another nightmare about Alice. She was riding a bull who was foaming at the mouth. Both of their eyes were red. The bull was charging at Delilah. She woke up with a start. *God, I wish I would stop having these nightmares!*

In the morning Delilah decided she was going to see her best friend no matter what! She drove over to the O'Doyle house. Eileen answered the door.

Hi.

It's not a good time, luv.

Delilah grabbed some courage and ran past Eileen. *I want to see her; I love her, Mrs. McCary, she's my best friend.* Delilah didn't stop running until she reached Alice's room.

Delilah was truly horrified when she saw Alice. She had a malevolent look on her face, her room stank, and she hissed at Delilah.

What's wrong with her?

Father Robert came into the room. *You shouldn't be here, Delilah!*

Why is she tied up, Father?

For everyone's safety, including hers.

What is wrong with her?

She's very sick, that's all I can say.

Elizabeth came into the room with Eileen. *I told you yesterday, Delilah, that Alice could not see you.*

GO AWAY, YOU LITTLE WHORE. WHAT'S WRONG, GOING TO CRY? GET OUT, YOU BITCH!
Delilah froze. That was not Alice talking. She did not know if the voice was female or male, but it was not Alice's. *What in God's name is happening?*
I AM A PIT DWELLER. I AM LEGION! YOU'RE NEXT! SO HOW IS THAT LITTLE FUCK MARKO?
Alice laughed hysterically.

Now it all made sense the dreams, the calls, everything. Did she do something to Marko? How could she, she was tied up. Everyone was silent.

Leave, Delilah, said Dr. Darby; *you don't need to see this.*
Delilah backed out of the room, and left.

Delilah's first thought was Facebooking Marko. She drove like the wind. When she got home she got on Facebook. She looked up Marko's profile, and texted him. Then she waited for a response, which took two hours. Marko texted from the hospital.

Sorry about missing our date, I was involved in a hit and run. My legs are broken in two places, and I'm pretty beat up!
Oh God, she hit him, but how? Delilah was in shock! She dropped her phone.

Delilah texted back and told Marko to tell her which hospital he was in so she could come and see him. Delilah was truly scared of Alice. *Is she going to do something to me?*

Delilah had to go see Marko in the hospital. She felt responsible for his accident.

Delilah's dad returned with a car. *Delilah, I have your rental. The guys from the body shop will pick your car up. Delilah? Delilah?*

Hi, Dad, I'm up in my room.

Her dad went upstairs.

What's up, honey? Why are you crying?

Dad I went to see Alice again.

Why did you do that?

I'm glad I did! I don't know what kind of sickness Alice has, Dad; she's evil!

Why do you say that?

She truly was frightening. I don't how to tell you this but they have her tied up.

Why would they do that?

They told me she could hurt me, or hurt herself.

Delilah went on to tell her dad that Father Robert was there, and Dr. Darby. Trip was mad.

I'm going to get to the bottom of this. I am going over to the O'Doyle house.

Dad, don't!

Somebody needs to answer for this. Trip left.

Trip knew he was speeding, but could not hold back. He reached the O'Doyle home in twenty minutes. He rang the doorbell, and waited on their porch. Eventually Ryan answered the door.

Trip, just go away, before I call the cops.

Good, have them come! You can explain why your daughter is tied up!

Go upstairs then.

I will.

Father Robert met him in the entrance way, saying, *Prepare yourself.*

Trip went raging up the stairs. Nothing could prepare him.

Alice, what's wrong, honey?

ALICE DOESN'T LIVE HERE ANYMORE.

What was wrong with her voice?

SHE IS WITH LEGION, INSIDE THIS BODY.

What?

GO AWAY, YOU FILTHY SWINE.

What's wrong with her, Ryan?

She is possessed, said Father Robert.

Trip looked around at everybody. *Like the movies?*

Yes, said Ryan.

My God! How?

They had a Ouija board, and that is an entrance to evil, said Father Robert.

Trip, we don't know for sure, but we think she played it with Delilah.

I don't understand!

Ken said, *Neither did I, until I treated her.*

LEGION WILL TAKE YOUR DAUGHTER TOO!

What's Legion?

WE ARE MANY!

Trip backed up. What he was looking at was evil; that much was for sure!

Please tell me how my daughter is involved!

Father Robert spoke up for the group. *It's a very long story. We could go into the people's experiences with the board, etc. Just look at her, and you will understand.*

SHE'S MINE, OLD MAN; YOUR CUNT OF A DAUGHTER IS NEXT. WE WILL ROT INSIDE HER! Alice laughed hysterically.

No you're not, you evil son of a bitch!

Trip and the group went downstairs to talk.

I am scared for Delilah!

If she needs any help, we're her to help, Trip, said Father Robert.

I just can't believe it! All over an Ouija board.

I would never have believed it myself, if I had not witnessed it, said Ken.

What's next?

Prayer, Trip, prayer.

Trip left the O'Doyle house horrified. He got into the car and drove away as fast as he came. *I won't let it happen to Delilah* – what if he could not stop it? Too unthinkable.

When Trip arrived, he was greeted by a horde of angry wasps. Trip tried to get away from them with little success. Where in God did they come from? His face and arms were covered in stings. Delilah looked out the front window in horror.

Trip finally got to the door. *Did you see those wasps?*

Of course I did, Dad; look at all those stings.

They hurt like hell. Got to get some calamine lotion.

They seemed to come out of nowhere, Dad.

I don't know where they came from, but like I said, it hurts like hell.

When they looked out the window, the wasps were gone.

Nightfall came and Delilah was scared.

Dad, can I sleep in you and Mom's room?

Sure, why not honey, bad day, hey!

She went into her room to change, and that'swhen saw Alice's demonic face at her window.

Holy shit!

The face disappeared. She ran into her dad's room.

Lord, I just saw Alice's face in my window, Dad.
You're overtired, and your mind plays all sort of tricks.
Sleep would not come easy tonight.
Shirley Shipley was active in the church, and a church fundraiser.
What happened to Delilah's car, Trip? she said, coming up the stairs. Delilah and Trip told Shirley the whole story.
I just can't believe it. That's why Father Robert was not at the fund raiser.
Back at the O'Doyle home, Elizabeth said, *We should check on Delilah; she is probably scared. I'll call Shirley in the morning.*
Everybody took a shift during the day; everyone had responsibilities for their day-to-day life. Alice required constant watching. She was sleeping, but for short periods at a time.
Ken and Father Robert were a Godsend to the family. Elizabeth realized she was falling in love again with Ken. She never thought he could be so selfless.
Ryan was watching Alice.
HOW DO YOU FEEL ABOUT YOUR WHORE OF A WIFE?! DID YOU NOT KNOW SHE HAS A WET CROTCH OVER HIM?
Ryan had become immune to the demon's cruelty, but that cut to the bone. Ryan lost it. *Shut your filthy mouth, you cruel demon.*
Father Robert was coming out of the bathroom when he heard Ryan.
Ryan, don't respond to it. He is a liar – he hates us humans.
I'm sorry; I should know better.

The demon preys on our weakness, Ryan. It is an enemy to the whole human race.

ADULTERY IS A SIN, PRIEST. SHE HAS INTENSE FEELINGS ABOUT HIS COCK.

Ryan left the room.

Ken and Elizabeth were sitting at the dining room table. Ryan's heart sank. He did not care how much blackmailing Mindy had in store, he was going to break off the relationship.

Hi, Ryan. Ryan, is it shift change? said Ken.

Please, Ken.

Okay, I will watch over her.

It's not Alice, so don't call it a girl.

Elizabeth jumped up, she was mad as hell. *Listen to me, Ryan! Our daughter is in there with it. Stop feeling sorry for yourself – you are not the only one suffering; we all are suffering. Alice is in there fighting for her soul.*

I'm sorry, Lizzy.

I'll go upstairs now, guys, said Ken.

Do you still love him, Lizzy?

I don't know, Ryan.

Please don't deny what I am going to ask you. You owe me this much.

Do you love Mindy?

NO! It's over, no matter what she does to me.

Okay! Yes I still love Ken. It's not the same as you and Mindy. All Ken has tried to do is help Alice and me in bad situations.

I know, but you're my wife, and Alice is my daughter.

I understand that, Ryan. I don't know what to feel anymore!

Ken walked into the room. Alice had soiled herself.

HOW SWEET I SMELL, DON'T YOU AGREE?
Ken never sponge-bathed Alice.
I HEAR EVERYTHING, SEE ALL YOUR SINS, KNOW HOW BAD YOU WANT TO BE INSIDE HER.
Ken ignored it as much as he could.
DO YOU KNOW HOW BAD SHE WANTS IT! HOW GOOD SHE SMELLS.
Ken was becoming mad.
WHAT'S THAT CUNT MINDY GOING TO SAY! GIVE ME MUSIC, HER MEMORIES TELL ABOUT A MANSON. THEY SAY HE IS THE ANTI-CHRIST SUPERSTAR. I THOUGHT THAT WAS LEGION'S DEPARTMENT. I WANT TO HEAR HIM, THROUGH THE PHONES.
Ken did nothing.
GOING TO BE THAT WAY – I'LL MAKE HER SUFFER!
I'll do it; just give me a chance.
Ken got her iPhone from Elizabeth. He tried to remember Alice's soul was still in there. He placed the earphones in Alice's ears, and played Marilyn Manson.
HE IS DIVINE, MY KIND OF GUY! THAT IS TRUE; I CAN SMELL THE SHIT ON THEIR KNEES.
Ken had started to pray; now that he knew the demon, he prayed a lot. *I hope Alice can hear one of her favorite artists in there.* He could remember her singing his songs. He really wasn't too bad of an artist.
Father Robert came to see Alice; he was a saint.
Hello, Father Robert said to Ken, *may God be with you.* He had come to like Ken very much. He could tell he had a pure soul.

It wanted to listen to the iPhone. The demon likes Marilyn Manson.

Well that does not surprise me.

Remember, Father, Alice loved him; you're not supposed to judge.

You are right, he said, embarrassed.

Father Robert talked to the Archbishop. The Archbishop had told him that there were no available priests; they were all busy with other cases. He told the Archbishop that a priest in Ireland was interested.

That was actually not really the case. He hoped Father Seamus would take the case, being that the demon wanted a war with him.

I will get in touch with the Archdiocese in Dublin, and see what we can do. We need an Exorcist for that poor girl.

Father Robert kissed the Archbishop's ring.

Father Robert began his shift. He began with silent prayer as usual. Father Robert sprinkled Holy Water on Alice.

IZGORILO. I WANT MORE MUSIC, OLD MAN, GIVE ME MUSIC.

Be quiet; again he used Holy Water.

IZGORILO, YOU COCKSUCKER!

Ryan came into the room.

Are you alright, Father?

Yes, yes, I just lost myself for a moment. I know Alice is in there some place. No priest for Exorcisms, too busy. This is insane. It's a sad day when you hear that.

Is Alice going to be able to rebuild after this?

Father Robert felt distraught. *Of course, we cannot lose faith, Ryan. God sees the pain Alice is going through. Many people have no memory of the possession.*

Really?

Yes really, Ryan.

That gives me hope.

Good. I will place another call in to Father Seamus. The Archbishop is trying his hardest.

Father Robert placed a call to Father Seamus. He wasn't there. He left a message.

Father Seamus, it's Father Robert from the States; please call.

Eileen was sitting with her granddaughter, or whatever it was. It was her shift with Alice.

TOP OF THE MORNING, CUNT.

Eileen was praying the rosary.

GIVE ME THOSE BEADS SO I CAN CHOKE YOU WITH THEM. DO YOU KNOW THAT COCKSUCKER KEN WANTS YOUR DAUGHTER'S CUNT?

Shut up, you devil.

WHAT'S WRONG, DID I PRESS A BUTTON, BITCH? I'D LIKE AN INVITATION TO THE WEDDING.

The demon knew it bothered Eileen that Ken loved Elizabeth.

I TOLD PATRICK HOW MUCH YOU MISSED HIM. HE WAS TOO BUSY SUCKING HILTER'S COCK. I LOVE SPENDING AN AFTERNOON WITH THE FUEHRER. HE STILL LIKES TO TORMENT, HELL OF A GUY. JUST LIKE YOUR DAUGHTER WOULD LIKE TO SUCK HER LOVER.

Eileen wanted to spit at it, but she knew Alice was in there someplace. Ken came to help her.

Mrs. McCary, I can watch Alice. It's too painful for you to keep going through this.

No thank you, Ken, but you could sit with me if you like.

Of course.

I do appreciate you being here. Father Robert tells me you care for my granddaughter very much.

I do.

Do you still love Elizabeth?

Very much, yes, and I was always very fond of Alice.

My hope is that my daughter is loved, by a good man.

Of course, Mrs. McCary.

Stop with Mrs. McCary, it's Eileen.

Okay, Eileen.

I know why she turned to you. I hate that Mindy. What do you two see in that woman? Everything is fake with her. I wish she would run off with a plastic surgeon! Her face is terrible with all that filler. She is evil too, just like this demon.

Ken was laughing at Eileen's comments.

I like your perspective. I don't love Mindy, I was just trying to hurt Ryan. It seems that I did not have all my facts straight.

Mindy will always have her men, Ken. She uses them like shoes, different pair each day.

Elizabeth, regardless of her addictions, is my soul mate, Eileen, and I'm not sorry about that.

I think I'm beginning to like you, Ken.

I have always liked you, Eileen, even if you didn't like me.

THIS CONVERSATION IS SOO SWEET! DO YOU WANT MOTHER AND DAUGHTER TIME, KEN? I'LL TELL PATRICK HIS WIFE HAS A NEW FUCK.

Was Patrick a good man? Did you love him?

Very much, Ken, although he had a wandering eye. That is probably why I've tolerated Ryan's affair. Some men can't help themselves.

If I had Elizabeth, I could help myself!

Maybe for a while.

When Father Robert got back the rectory, Father Seamus called.

Father, I am so glad you called!

How's the girl?

She is the same; there is a great team working with her.

Did you say there was a doctor present?

There are two doctors present. A medical doctor, and a psychiatrist.

What does the psychiatrist think?

He thought a lot of things, but he has seen mental illness a lot. It does not feel like a mental illness.

His understanding is paramount to the case.

We have no priests available for Exorcisms; they are all working on other cases.

No priests at all? What?

How many Exorcists are there in Dublin?

That is true.

Will you come if the church gives its approval?

Of course.

Thank you, Father Seamus.

To Father Seamus that was a lot of priests busy in the field. He knew, always knew, this Exorcism was his job.

Elizabeth called Shirley.

Hi Shirley, sorry I haven't called sooner.

What is happening, Elizabeth?

Have you talked to Trip, Shirley?

Trip and Delilah, I can't believe it!

It's true, please keep it to yourself.

How is Delilah?

Scared!

I'm sure she is.

Can I come by, Elizabeth?

It's not a good idea, I appreciate it though.

Well if there's anything I can do, I will.

I'll call you if I need anything.

We care, Elizabeth.

Thank you; goodbye, Shirley.

Ryan had lost twenty pounds; he was skinny. Everyone had lost weight, especially Father Robert. He kept fasting to keep himself in a state of grace. He spent a lot of time with Alice.

YOU AGAIN, PRIEST, I DESPISE YOU. I CAN'T WAIT TILL YOU'RE IN HELL. WE WILL TORMENT YOU IN HELL LIKE YOU HAVE TORMENTED ME.

Father Seamus is coming.

GOOD, WE WILL HAVE OUR DEBT REPAID.

We will drive you out. A fly landed on Alice and tried to fly away. The demon lunged forward and ate it.

I LOVE FLIES, DON'T YOU, FATHER?

Father Robert gagged.

I WOULD LIKE MORE PLEASE.

Ken and Eileen were trying to make a go of it for Alice.

Ken, please take me for a walk, just to get away for a while.

Sure.

The fall was beautiful in New York.

I feel guilty, Ken, saying this but, I wish I were back in Dublin.

Is that so wrong? If you wished you were here, I'd be treating you as a patient.

You just might need to do that.

Do you believe in God, Ken?

Yes, I do now.

Good, he will not let Alice suffer for long.

I hope not. Do you think she knows what's happening, Ken?

No, she is in there though – I think she hides from it like children playing hide and seek, only she hides.

You're the best in the field for a reason.

Ryan was having the toughest time of all. He was supposed to be Alice's protector. He could not stand the sight of his daughter. He was very ashamed.

Elizabeth picked up on this and tried to be there with him when he was with Alice.

Ryan, would you like me to go with you when you watch Alice?

I will be turning to morphine myself if you don't! I can understand now why you used it to get away.

Not anymore, I still have pain – but I will never sink that low again.

Lizzy, I still want us to work. I know I have made mistakes, but I want to have a chance to prove myself.

It might be too late.

Is it because of Ken?

NO! I have been hurt too much. Everything in my life has changed. You brought that broad into our lives, even when I told you not to.

Father Robert came to tell them that Father Seamus might be coming over from Dublin. They all knew now that there were no available priests in their Archdiocese. The demon wanted Father Seamus. The one across the sea.

Ken came over to relieve Ryan and Elizabeth, both of whom were happy to see him.

I brought take-out.

That's great, Ken, said Ryan and Elizabeth. *Big fat juicy sandwiches.*

They sat down for lunch and had a feast. It was a pleasant surprise.

They had to set up an I.V. for Alice. If anyone was to see their day-to-day life, they would not understand the reasoning behind their decisions.

Elizabeth went to take her shift. She still needed to take the Percodan, and Oxytocin, especially under the circumstances. She was not mainlining.

COMING TO SIT WITH YOUR SWEET CHILD, ARE YOU?

You're not my child!

WE HATE YOU, AND YOUR LITTLE BITCH. SHE IS WARM, SO WE ARE ENJOYING EVERY MOMENT.

Father Seamus is coming.

WELL, WE WELCOME THE VISIT. OLD FRIEND WILL LOSE THIS WAR; WE HAVE BEEN WAITING FOR HIM. DEBTS NEED TO BE REPAID.

Elizabeth had not been there much for her daughter. Now Alice was paying the price. Lizzy was holding out hope for Father Seamus.

Today it was a lot harder for her to be around Alice. She was very tired of pulling double shifts. Why did Ryan have to be the way he was? Distant from the whole situation.

Ryan was still taking a break in his and Lizzy's room.

Ryan? Ryan? Come on, Ryan, it's your turn as well.

I know, I am coming. Ryan was getting a Xanax.

Ken had written the prescription. He needed something to relieve his nerves. Why had he bought the board? He had no idea why. It was a lark. How could he know evil would come to his door? His mother had given him the St. Michael's medallion. He had a hard time believing God would allow his daughter to suffer so.

Alice was asleep when Ryan went into the room. Elizabeth was crying.

What's the matter, Lizzy?

She looks peaceful when she sleeps. I hope she can hear our prayers.

A year ago, I would have transferred the patient to Ken, if the patient were Alice.

Alice was twitching her body in her sleep.

Do you think that's Alice?

Yes, it's her fighting for her soul, said Lizzy.

Father Robert was waiting for a decision about Alice. He rarely slept or ate. This was eating away his soul. He hoped Father Seamus would come quickly. He didn't know how long it would be.

CHAPTER FOUR

FATHER SEAMUS

Father Seamus always knew he would be a priest. As a child some dreams were so beautiful. Others were worse than nightmares. He always had a dream about a man on fire with no eyes. He would continue to dream this dream when he became a priest. Father Seamus never thought he would be an Exorcist – until he met Shawna McClellan.

She changed his life. Shawna was a lovely girl from County Clare, Ireland. She had terrible fits at school. One day her desk levitated to the ceiling. She had to leave school; she was scaring the children. Her parents kept her home after that. The medical community was at a loss. Her parents were devout Catholics, and they had turned to the church.

Father Seamus came to see her, and put on a St. Michael's medallion. She let out a wail like a banshee. He did not know what was happening until Sister Mary told him Shawna was possessed. She had been involved in an Exorcism years ago, and she never got over it. She trained Father Seamus. There was no time for him to go to the Vatican to be trained. Sister Mary was a hyper-sensitive. She knew as soon as she met Shawna.

The Exorcism lasted ten months. They demon finally gave him a name, and was cast out. After the Exorcism, he had kept in touch with Sister Mary. He needed her now, and so he called her.

Hello, Sister Mary speaking.

Hello Sister Mary.

Hello, luv.

Father Seamus here.

I be knowing your voice after all these years.

Sister Mary, can we have a cup of tea at the rectory?

I be knowing why you be a-calling. It is about the girl from the States.

You always had the second sight.

I had some terrible nightmares about her. You will be a-needing me for this one.

Sister Mary, you are sixty-six years old.

Not too old to be fighting for souls. You will be a-needing me for this one.

I be needing approval from the Archdiocese.

You'll be a-getting it.

Sister Mary was a very devoted nun. She and grown up in County Clare and had the perfect childhood. Her mother was going to be a nun until she met David O'Donald. Their life was idyllic, and even more so when Mary came. Mary was visited by the Mother of God when she was a child. She did not know who she was until she spoke.

I will always be with you; you are called to walk with Christ, as I am his Mother. She told her mother; she was three. Her mother took her to the church to see Father Sean.

You see that man on the cross, that's Mary's son; our lord Jesus Christ.

She wanted to walk with the Lord. She became a nun when she was twenty. Forty-six years she had served the Lord.

Tis a big one this, Sister Mary said.

Why do you say that? All of them are horrid.

This be a strong demon.

All of them are strong.

You know there be geography in hell. This demon be high in Satan's court. That's what I saw in me dreams now for a fortnight, Sister Mary explained.

Well, you got the gift.

If you want to call it that.

Father Seamus went to the Archdiocese office, and Archbishop McCrae saw him. The Archbishop had news.

If you see fit to it, do the Exorcism.

Well I think it be my case anyways.

He called Father Robert.

Father Robert, it be me, Father Seamus.

Yes, Father.

I'll be coming to do the Exorcism.

Father Seamus was very tired. He needed sleep. He dreamt of hell. He was standing in front of a bog, when an incubus approached him.

You can't win always, Father. This time we take the maggot to the pit.

Father Seamus woke up with a start. He leaped out of bed, grabbed some Holy Water, and sprinkled his rectory with it. He always did this when he descended into hell.

Our Father who – he grabbed his head; it was throbbing so hard he could barely see. He continued on with the prayer, and it finally it ceased. This was terrifying, but he was going to be facing more terrifying times in a short while.

Morning could not come fast enough.

In the morning Mr. McGee came banging on the rectory door.

Father, come quickly, you won't believe this.

What's all the commotion about, Mr. McGee?

Father Seamus went to see what Mr. McGee was on about.

Come outside, Father.

Father Seamus went outside with Mr. McGee. To both of their shock, the oak tree was filled with crows.

What in the name of our Lord is that, Father? How can the branches support all the weight, Father?

Go inside, McGee, they're heading our way.

They slammed the rectory door. Hundreds of birds were coming. They were slamming the wall outside the rectory.

Dear God help us was all they could say. It seemed like the attack lasted hours. They waited it out.

Do ya think it's over, Father?

The only way to know is to go outside and check.

I'll be doing it, Father.

Mr. McGee went outside, and he came back gagging.

What's wrong, Mr. McGee?

Don't be going outside – it-it's a terrible sight.

Father Seamus went anyway.

Outside were the crows, and out of their eyes came fire ants. Father Seamus was shocked. Father Seamus knew it was another sign, but he kept it to himself. It was the demon's way of telling Father Seamus he was ready for battle. Well that's fine, so was he.

It wasn't like Father Seamus was not scared; he was. Possession always felt so wrong to Father Seamus, the vilest assault against mankind.

Father Seamus returned to the rectory. There he would have a violent vision. There was a red-haired girl with reptilian green eyes. Her red hair was matted and she had a red gash for a mouth. She was on the ceiling upside down. She dropped down on Father Seamus – the vision was over. This girl was much worse than Shawna. He now knew what he needed to be prepared for. Father Robert said the Lord's Prayer.

Elizabeth was in Alice's room watching her. Alice began to levitate to the ceiling. Elizabeth was dumbfounded. How was she doing it?

Alice? Alice!

Alice reached the ceiling and hung upside down.

Good God, help me!

MOTHER, I CAN FLY, crackled the demon.

Elizabeth screamed for Father Robert.

He was there in an instant.

What is it doing?

I don't know!

Father Robert held up the St. Michael's medallion, and Alice dropped down on the bed. Everybody ran to the room.

Eileen, go get the rope right now, said Ken.

Everybody else held Alice down. It was hard, to say the least.

What happened? asked Ken and Ryan.

She just started to float to the ceiling, and hung upside down. She dropped down to the bed when Father Robert showed her the St. Michael's medallion.

They were speechless.

I need to get more Holy Water, said Father Robert after a long silence.

Ryan said, *Lizzy, I never will leave you or Eileen alone on shift – Ken, Father Robert, or I will be there. We will start sleeping in here. Everyone together okay?*

Everyone agreed.

They all were asleep when they heard Biggie Smalls moaning loudly. Ken was the first to wake up; what he was seeing was impossible. The demon was trying to eat Biggie Smalls. Alice's mouth was opened like a very large snake, and she was trying to swallow him.

Father Robert poured Holy Water on Alice. She spat Biggie Smalls out of her mouth, and shrieked.

IZGORILO, hissed the demon. *YOU FUCKING CUNT PRIEST, YOU'LL PAY FOR THAT, MAGGOT!*

The demon broke through the restraints and was free once again. It lunged at Father Robert and bit him in the leg. He shrieked in pain. Ryan and Ken were trying their hardest to break the demon free from Father Robert.

Grab the Holy Water for the love of God, cried Father Robert.

Ken grabbed the water and ran it down Alice's face. Father Robert passed out.

Every one of them was terrified; what else was coming?

Eileen was grabbed by the hair and dragged down the hallway to the bathroom. The demon pushed her face into the toilet and flushed.

Ryan, Ken, and Elizabeth went with a cross and branded the demon with it.

IZGORILO!

They all jumped on Alice, then dragged her back to her room.

I thought it would drown me; I have never been more afraid in me life.

The demon had regained its power and turned on Ken; it was trying to choke the life out of him.

YOU'LL NEVER GET IT UP HER ASS AGAIN, MAGGOT.

Ryan quickly grabbed the St. Michael's medallion. *Look at it, you son of a bitch!*

Alice fell. Ken and Ryan retied the rope.

Ryan ran to Father Robert as he was coming to.

Father!

Father Robert was in agony.

Ken, can you watch Father Robert while I get a shot of morphine for him?

Ken was winded but was able to help.

Father Robert, I am going to give you a shot of morphine for the pain. Now you need to let me examine you. I need to see the injury you sustained; please, everyone, give the man his privacy.

Everyone left but Ryan and Father Robert, so Ryan could evaluate his injury.

Father Robert was glad he had the morphine shot.

It's really not so bad, Ryan.

That's the 10-mg shot of morphine; you should be lying flat on the floor!

Father Robert had a beautiful vision of Mary, the Mother of God. *You are halfway through the road you're on, don't falter.* Then it went black.

The demon became very quiet. It was too quiet, and malevolent looking.

Ryan had also given Alice 10 mg of morphine, but she didn't go to sleep. Everyone but Father Robert had regained their energy – Father Robert was blissfully sleeping. They reattached her I.V.

I HAD FUN. I PLAYED A GAME! NOW IT'S TIME TO RUN AWAY – THIS OLD MAN CAME ROLLING HOME!

It was Alice's voice – then she slept.

We all must rest in shifts. Lizzy and I will take the first watch; everyone else will rest, Ryan said.

No resistance from Eileen or Ken. As parents would with any sick child, they stayed together.

How long will it take for Father Seamus to come over from Ireland?

I don't know, Lizzy. When Father Robert is better we'll ask.

Is he going to be alright?

Yes, I'll watch for infection.

What happened to us, Ryan?

I don't know? I spent too much time at work, you took too many pills, I just don't know, Lizzy.

Also Mindy and Ken.

Will you leave me for him? I don't know; that's the honest truth.

I am not trying to make your mind up, but Alice really is going to need our help after this.

I know, Ryan; that's why I can't make a decision.

I'm going to check on Father Robert.

Father Robert was awake, he must have heard them.

Hi, Father Robert, how are you feeling now?

I know this sounds very strange: I feel happy.

No, that's perfectly normal, it's the morphine, laughed Ryan.

Oh, I see, Ryan.

You're high, Father.

Well, I guess this is what all the fuss is about.

You said it, not me. They laughed.

Do you know when Father Seamus is coming?

Soon I hope.

He will make Alice better?

Yes, of course, he hoped. *Once the church does the paperwork, I am sure Father Seamus will be on his way.*

Elizabeth went to check on her mother and Ken. They were fast asleep. Watching Ken sleep made her feel happiness for a while.

Elizabeth, is that you watching me?

Caught in the act.

Come lie down with me, Elizabeth?

I wish I could, Ken, but it's wrong.

Elizabeth went to Ken anyway.

God, Ken, I want your touch.

Elizabeth, it feels so good to hold you.

Your love has carried me through this, Ken. I came to check on my mother; she needs me.

Sorry, Elizabeth, check on your mother.

Mom, you sleeping?

Eileen never moved.

I'll let you sleep, Mother.

Can we talk, Elizabeth?

Yes, Ken?

Have you thought about us?

Yes, many times, but it's not the time.

I just wanted to know that you had thought about it.

I think about you all the time, Ken.

Ken went to Elizabeth and kissed her.

You sleep; Lizzy; Ryan and I need to come up with another medication schedule.

I do love you, Ken; that's why it is so hard to make a decision.

Ryan had fallen asleep in the chair. Alice was behind the rocking chair.

Ryan, wake up!

What?

Oh shit!

How did she get out of her restraints?

Alice? Alice? Is that you?

ALICE DOESN'T LIVE HERE ANYMORE.

Christ, Ken, help me.

Ken walked very slowly up to Alice.

Get the morphine right now, Ryan!

The needle from the last injection was still by the bed. Ryan grabbed the morphine and injected. The demon just stared from behind the chair; nothing happened! Ryan and Ken both tackled her.

Okay, Alice, let's get back into bed.

76

Ryan and Ken put her back to bed. She was surprisingly content.

It's too quiet, Ken.

Let's just be happy about that, okay?

I'M JUST WAITING ON A FRIEND, sang Alice.

Ryan and Ken just stood there.

SOON THE LITTLE FUCKER WILL BE HERE.

Alice fell asleep.

That was too close for my liking.

Mine too, Ryan. I know this is the wrong time, but we need to talk about Elizabeth.

Lizzy is MY wife!

I know but that does not stop me from loving her.

Alice needs her parents, especially right now.

What about Mindy, Ryan? I just can't take away my feelings for her, Ryan.

I am not asking you to do that, just leave it for now.

I can't, Ryan. We need a plan of action for Alice so this doesn't happen anymore.

Staying awake would be first.

It's not your fault, we're all exhausted.

What do you think this priest Father Seamus can do, Ken?

I don't know? Maybe just maybe he will – this coming from a former atheist.

Yeah, I know what you mean.

How do two men of science define this?

We need to look at the world in a different light, Ken.

Yes indeed, Ryan. I have dealt with a lot of bad people, Ryan – it's a part of what I do.

You mean your forensics patients?

Yes, but not this kind of evil.

Christ, what is left of Alice gets less everyday, Ken.

I know, Ryan.

The demon was stirring.

GOOD FUCKING MORNING, FAGGOTS, TAKE THIS BOTHERSOME BAG AWAY!

It's an I.V.; she needs it to live, you demonic monster.

I HAVE MET SOME OF YOUR PATIENTS. EVIL- SOME, ARE THEY NOT, KEN? RANDY CHAMBERS AND I WATCHED HIS BITCH OF A WIFE BURNING FROM HIS BLOWTORCH. WE WERE GOING TO ROAST WEENIES OVER HER. WHEN WILL SEAMUS BE HERE TO PAY HIS DEBTS?

Will you leave then?

NO, DADDY! I HAVE FRIENDS OF MINE WHO WOULD LIKE TO MEET HER. JUST REMEMBER I AM DEATH AND DESTRUCTION. WHEN FATHER SEAMUS COMES, WITH HIS VIRGIN BITCH, DEBTS WILL BE REPAID.

I LOVED WATCHING YOUR VINCENT KEM- PLING. HE WAS A PROTÉGÉ OF MINE. HACKING OFF THE VICTIMS' FINGERS ONE AT A TIME, WHILE THEY WATCHED.

Ken lost it this time. *Shut your fucking mouth!*

Don't talk to it. This is what it wants, our attention. Who is Vincent Kempling?

A recent patient of mine. Sociopath of the worst kind. It's true he cut off each finger one by one, while the victim watched!

That is truly horrid. How can you be around these people?

It's my job – this demon is worse. I never thought people could become possessed, Ryan. Now it will be hard to go back to work; things won't be the same.

CHAPTER FIVE

THE ARCHDIOCESE

Mr. McGee drove both Father Seamus and Sister Mary to the airport. The church knew Sister Mary's expertise in such cases – the church gave her their blessing. As they crossed the Irish Sea, they flew into a terrible storm that came on suddenly.

Tis a violent one this is, Father Seamus, tis a warning I think.

I agree with ya. What are we going into, Sister?

As I said before, there is a hierarchy in hell. This demon is high in the order. This will be much stronger of a demon. Prepare and pray is all we can do.

Well, Sister, your heart is pure.

So is yours, Seamus.

Back in New York, Delilah was having fits of anger.

She wore all black, and listened to a lot of Iron Maiden –
loudly. Shirley Shipley was very worried.

What happened to you going to the hospital to see Marko?

He's a goof, sports queer, I'll never go out with a jock.

What about Alice?

She is a fucking freak, I am not hanging out with a lunatic!

*She is very sick, Delilah; I don't really know what's wrong
with Alice.*

Father Seamus and Sister Mary had two separate
living accommodations. Sister Mary was staying with
the nuns, while Father Seamus was staying with Father
Robert. Father Robert was still recovering from the
demon's bite.

Ryan, Ken, and Father Robert picked them up after their
long journey. They were holding signs up to greet them.

*Good Morning, Father Seamus. We are very happy to see
you.*

Happy to help, this is Sister Mary.

Hello, nice to be meeting ya.

Should we go see Alice?

No I will need to see the Archbishop.

Sister Mary must go to the Sisters.

Sure, we are just very excited to see you.

*I need to have a Black Fast, which is three days long. Sister
Mary will also have to fast for three days with the Sisters.
Father Robert will be there assisting.*

I heard about his injury. You treated him yourself?

Yes I did, Father.

Sister Mary has had experience with Exorcisms.

That's good to know.

You have made a diagnosis, Dr. Darby.

There is no diagnosis; she's beyond a diagnosis. There really is no mental illness.

We need to rest while we can; there will be an ongoing assault. Try to do the same.

We are sleeping in shifts.

Good, just be patient; this is a war, you have seen nothing yet.

Ryan and Ken drove to Father Robert's rectory.

Father, tell me about the girl.

She is truly terrifying!

They all are, Father Robert.

It won't give me a name.

It won't until it has to leave.

It said it is with Legion!

They all are, Father. How are you feeling?

Good but I think it's the pain medication.

You will have to be off it for the Exorcism. You need a sharp mind, no drugs.

Okay, Father, let me tell you about the girl!

Sister Mary arrived at the nuns' residence.

You are most welcome, Sister Mary, said Sister Veronica.

The Sisters all wanted to hear about the girl.

I have never met the girl. It does not matter, a demon is a demon. No matter how high they are in Satan's Court.

Would you like something to eat?

Yes, please, then I will need to fast for three days. I like to build my energy first. We will have to wait a bit for the Exorcism.

Father Robert will need more time; let's eat, Sister Mary.

They had a great feast of roast beef and potatoes.

At the rectory, Father Robert began to fast; he wanted

to be prepared. The pain medication was affecting his appetite.

How did this all come about again, Father Robert?

Alice was playing with an Ouija board.

They are horrible entry points, Father Robert.

I know but the father bought the board; he regrets it dearly.

Yes, no judgments, we are all sinners. What can you tell me about Alice?

She was an honor student, but always a little morbid. There's a poet named Slyvia Plath, she gassed herself in the same house as her children slept.

She was a great poet, Father Robert.

Well, Alice loves her poetry.

They both fasted and rested before meeting Alice.

Father Robert, I'm ready to meet the girl. I need to contact the Sisters to have Sister Mary be at the meeting.

The Sisters were very excited to meet Father Seamus.

He's just a man, not a God, Sisters!

They were embarrassed about their demeanor.

Ryan picked them up.

I feel hope now, Father Seamus, I am really a changed man.

Good, we'll need it.

They headed to the O'Doyle house. As soon as they got there Sister Mary had a vision of the demon. It was a very powerful one indeed.

Prepare yourself, Father. I don't be knowing the name, but it is up high.

Sister Mary knew as soon as she as she saw the house; there was a black bubble around it. Sister Mary was very scared, as scared as she ever had been.

It's awful, Father.

They all are, let's say the Saint Michael prayer.

They all prayed their own private prayers as well.

No time like the present, Sister. I'll be coming.

As soon as they got into the house they smelled sulfur.

Let's see the girl.

Do you want to meet my family?

After we see the girl.

Her name is Alice.

She's the host, I mean the demon.

They entered her room; the demon had removed its restraints again. She was just sitting in the rocking chair. Even Father Seamus was shocked.

Let's restrain her again.

YOU KNOW THERE REALLY IS NO NEED AS YOU CAN SEE, BASTARDS. I COME AND I GO QUITE EASILY.

They restrained her anyway.

Who are you, demon? Give me your name.

IT IS FORBIDDEN; YOU SHOULD KNOW, OLD FRIEND.

That means I've cast you out before.

NOT ME, FRIENDS OF MINE, I STAY IN THE SWINE, YOU WILL NOT DEFEAT ME.

Father Robert came to the house.

I need to be here, Elizabeth.

I understand, but my husband won't.

I will go up to see Alice, as always. I can't sit on the side, I need to do it, Elizabeth. Show the demon I am strong.

Go up, Father.

Father Robert went to the room. It smelled like something was burning.

What is that, Father Seamus?

It is just another trick by the demon. Why are you here, demon?

SHE CALLED, I CAME.

You'll leave, said Sister Mary.

LOOK, IT'S FATHER SEAMUS'S CUNT.

I AM SURE YOU'VE SEEN HERS, FATHER.

Father Seamus sprinkled her with Holy Water.

IZGORILO!

I know you speak Latin.

YES, BUT SO DO YOU, NO FUN.

I will be successful at casting you out.

FATHER ROBERT, YOU'RE BACK, GOOD TO SEE YOU, CUNT!

I am just fine, you did not defeat me.

WE KNEW YOU WERE COMING; THAT'S WHY THEY SENT ME. YOU WILL NOT SEND ME TO THE PIT.

Yes we will, said Father Robert.

THIS TIME WE WIN!

The room was burning hot.

Stop the tricks – no one is impressed.

The closet door flew open. There was a fiery tunnel with hundreds of demons devouring lost souls.

Tis only a trick of the mind, said Sister Mary.

IT'S THERE – HOW DO YOU THINK I GOT UP?

The doors in the house all slammed. Ken came to the house in time to hear the commotion.

I'm going, Elizabeth; they will need my help.

Okay, Ken.

As soon as the demon saw him, it growled.

Hi everybody, bad time.

YOU LITTLE FUCK, COME TO SEE YOUR WHORE.
Ken ignored the demon.
DO YOU KNOW HE'S FUCKING THE WIFE?
Silence! I will be back, and you will leave! said Father
Seamus. *Keep the child restrained, the demon strength is pow-*
erful but it goes on and off. I would like to meet the family now.
Father Seamus and Sister Mary went to meet the family.
It's not just her that needs help, this house needs a blessing.
You two warring in this house, over a married woman? You are
doctors; act like them, said Sister Mary.
All who are Catholic will need to go to confess your sins,
then take the Blood and Body of Christ.
Ken was the only one not Catholic. He said private
prayers for Alice. They went back to the room.
The room began to smell like a barn. Alice's eyes
rolled back in her head, and she began to moan. The
demon had a pair of scissors in its hand rocking in the
rocking chair. There was red hair all over the room. She
had cut her matted hair – she sat there laughing.
DO I LOOK PRETTY?
Eileen gasped – she was the only one who ever cut
Alice's hair. She had been doing it since Alice was a child.
Look what she did to her bleeding hair.
DO YOU WANT ME TO CUT YOURS?
Eileen went silent.
Can you give her anything to slow her down?
No. We have to wait.
The demon lunged at Father Seamus, drove the scis-
sors into his leg.
God in heaven!
The demon laughed loudly.

Help him, Ryan?

The demon backed away from the group.

DON'T ANY OF YOU MAGGOTS TOUCH ME.

Father Robert sprinkled the demon with Holy Water.

IZGORILO, YOU FUCKING FAGGOT.

It was enough to slow it down. They all grabbed her. She tussled with them all.

Jesus help us, cried Father Robert.

There was a smell of roses hovering in the room.

Get her restrained, men, cried Father Seamus.

You need to get tougher restraints.

They doubled up the rope.

Be tough but remember it is still Alice.

Demon, give me your name, shouted Father Seamus.

FUCK OFF, PRIEST!

Give me a name!

MR. ROGERS, the demon crackled.

Enough! Everyone leave the room except Father Robert and Sister Mary.

Father Seamus, Father Robert, and Sister Mary recited The Lord's Prayer.

I will be returning for the Exorcism!

They all sprinkled Alice with Holy Water.

IZGORILO!

It's burning it; Alice will feel no pain, only the demon will. When we return there will be no refuge for you, demon, and you come out of this godly girl.

NEVER, YOU PRICK!

We will return, demon!

Father Seamus and the others sat at the dining room table.

We will return, and I will cast out this demon.

Does anyone have questions?

Father Seamus, how long will the Exorcism take? asked Eileen.

That depends on many things. Firstly, Sister Mary said he is high in Satan's Court. How high and which demon is the question. We will find out at the Exorcism. Father Robert will be assisting me. He needs to mend still. I have gone as long as a year, but don't let that discourage you.

A year, said Ken and Ryan. They both had practices to go back to.

That's right, gentlemen! I will stay until the demon is cast out. It was nice meeting you all, but I need to go to see the Archbishop.

Ryan drove them to the Archdiocese. Father Seamus's leg hurt like hell, but he would not take anything for it.

The Archdiocese office gladly welcomed the visit. Archbishop McKean saw them in his office.

Have you met the girl, Father Seamus?

I just came from their house. The demon is high in Satan's Court. This is what we discovered, he of course is with Legion. Possibly a right hand demon to Satan.

Oh Lord, we will have to be extremely careful.

I am always careful, Archbishop McKean.

How did this come about?

Ouija board, they sell them at many toy stores.

I did not know that!

Passed himself off as a lonely teenage boy. Alice and her girlfriend invited it to show himself and he did.

How's the other girl?

Fine, no reports of activity.

Check on the other girl!

Yes, your excellence.

They left the office in good spirits. This should start very soon.

Who is the other girl, Father Robert?

A girl named Delilah Shipley; her mother is very devout. I have her address and phone number at the rectory. Let's go there for a start.

They went back to the rectory and found the address.

Best to go over, watch their body language very closely.

They left for the Shipley home. Their escort was Father Patrick, who was glad to be of service in these trying times.

God will surely reward your devotion to this case, Father Patrick.

It is my honor, Father Seamus.

All this attention, I will start getting a fat head.

I also admire Sister Mary and of course Father Robert.

Thank you, my son, said Sister Mary.

Yes, thank you, Father Patrick. Let's go to the girl's house, Father Patrick.

They retrieved the address from the rectory, headed to the Shipley house, and rang the bell. Delilah, all decked out in Goth attire, answered the door.

My Mom's not home, said Delilah, then closed the door in their faces. They were shocked and rang again.

Dad, get the door, it's some Jesus lovers at our door.

Trip answered the door.

Hi there, Fathers and Sister.

Father Robert spoke first. *Hello, Mr. Shipley, can we have a moment of your time?*

Certainly, but my wife's not home.

You will be fine, said Father Robert.

Come in then.

This is regarding your lovely daughter, they said facetiously.

Delilah? What about Delilah? Is she in trouble? Please come have a seat, Fathers, Sister.

Well best to head on with it. We have come to talk to you about Alice O'Doyle.

Oh I see, where would you like to start?

With your daughter if that's okay?

Of course! Delilah get down here – he was tired of her behavior.

What?

They want to talk to you about Alice.

Delilah begrudgingly came down.

What do you want to know?

She's your best friend since first grade, right, Delilah?

No, she is a fucking loon.

Trip slapped her across the face.

I have had enough of your behavior.

Delilah was shocked.

What do you want to know?

We want to talk to you about the Ouija board.

Why?

Did you use it?

Yeah!

Stop the attitude, Delilah!

Why, Dad? Big deal, some little queer boy named Brian called me a slut!

Tis never any boy Delilah, added Sister Mary.

Whatever!

You are very cheeky, said Sister Mary.

Father Seamus gave her a stern look.

We need to know if you have had any problems lately?

Her attitude for starts, then her attire and music!

Is this recently?

Yes!!

Oh Dad, shut up.

God in heaven, are you sassy, girl! chirped Sister Mary.

You're a fat bitch.

Your car goes today, Delilah – take the bus! Trip was completely fed up.

No! I'm very sorry.

No go, Delilah! It's mine until you are sociable with people!

Do you know that you can become like Alice?

Why?

You used the board, shouted Father Seamus.

Really?

Really!

I'm not like Alice!

When did her behavior change, Mr. Shipley?

A month ago, she has been more aggressive in the last two weeks.

She is under oppression, Mr. Shipley.

Please tell me what that means?

She's under attack! cried Sister Mary.

What?

Really, you guys; Delilah was afraid.

Yes, said the Fathers.

Delilah cried.

Yes, missy, you should be a-crying! shouted Father Seamus.

If I were you, I be a-praying as we speak, added Sister Mary.

What can I do?

Get to church. We will give you a blessing that should help.

Fuck off!

Delilah!

They're Jesus freaks, Dad!

We're your saviors, Delilah!

Maybe ya should leave.

Sister Mary discreetly placed a cross behind Delilah's back.

Delilah let out a wail.

Ya see that, Mr. Shipley?

Maybe you should stay!

Delilah, what's wrong, honey?

It hurts in my back!

It travels up the spine, Trip.

Is that right, Father Robert?

Listen to them; they're experts.

Do ya know how many young girls we have seen under oppression in my time?

Father Seamus, you are telling me what?

I'm telling ya, man, your daughter's soul hangs in the balance.

Dear God!

We need to get back to the Archbishop, Trip. Give him an update.

Wait for my wife, Shirley; this should be a joint decision.

Thank you, Trip.

Shirley was home within an hour.

Shirley, Father Robert and the others would like to talk to you.

Goodness, how long have you been waiting?

About an hour, Ma'am, said Sister Mary.

It's about Delilah.

Well she's right there.

No, Ma'am, about the behavior.

Her behavior has been very poor for a month or so.

She is under attack, Ma'am. Did you have her baptized?

Yes! Father Robert baptized her.

Good, Ma'am. She will need to take confession and have the Body and Blood of our Lord.

Yes, Sister Mary.

Try three times a week.

No way, you Jesus freak!

Delilah Marie Shipley! I don't understand. Do you understand, Trip?

Not really.

Are you bloody deaf, man! She may become just like Alice.

Good God, Trip!

I'm sorry, Trip, said Father Seamus.

We're as serious as a heart attack, added Father Robert.

We will do it starting tonight. Father Kevin is saying Mass at six; then he will need her confession. Confess everything you have done, including the board, Delilah.

She will; I am going to bring her myself.

Thank you, Trip.

Alice remained the same. If anything she was getting worse. Her room always smelled foul, and she was very violent. She had started to rip her nails off, and was breaking her teeth on the bed railing. She became more hideous every day.

Elizabeth and Eileen were on night shift. They walked into her room when Alice was pulling out her eyelashes.

Stop it, said Elizabeth.

STILL TRYING TO SAVE THE CHILD?

Always.

SHE IS A PIECE OF SCUM.

Fuck off!

Eileen walked into the room.

Stop your swearing; it does no good.

I just want this to be over!

Elizabeth, we all want that.

When is it going to happen?

You heard what Father Seamus said; it could be up to a year.

I cannot wait a year.

You will have no choice.

Ken came into the room.

Ladies, this does not help; it just gets a kick out of it.

Ryan was in the kitchen when Trip called.

How bad is it?

Very bad.

They think Delilah's something called oppressed, Ryan.

What does that mean?

Whatever it is, it's bad! We're going to church at six. I'm sorry, Ryan; I need a favor.

What?

Ryan, can we see Alice one more time?

Tomorrow morning sound okay?

Sure, thanks, Ryan.

Tomorrow sounded like a long time.

Trip, Shirley, and Delilah came early in the morning.

Ryan answered the door. *Hi guys, come in.*

Thank you so much, Ryan, said Trip.

Yes, said Shirley, *thank you.*

Delilah just looked scared. She had not dressed herself in Goth attire.

Ken and Elizabeth are with her now; go up.

Nothing could prepare them.

YOU'RE SCARED!

What do you want with our daughter? yelled Shirley.

IT'S NOT ME THAT WANTS SOMETHING, IT'S THE OTHERS.

I'm sorry I used the board.

WE ARE NOT SORRY YOU USED THE BOARD, SLUT.

Leave us alone, shouted Trip.

THE OTHERS WILL NOT, YOU OLD FOOL.

They could not see Alice anymore; they only saw evil. They left the room.

Elizabeth, it's good to see you, said Shirley.

I wish it was under better terms.

How do you cope?

You just have to in order to not go mad.

We miss you so much, Elizabeth.

I truly believe this has strengthened our faith, Shirley.

What can we do for you?

Keep Delilah safe.

Trip approached Ryan.

Ryan, can we talk?

Sure, Trip.

I've never been so afraid in my life.

Trip, it hasn't happened yet. It may never happen.

I don't think I could go through what you're going through.

You still have time to change it – what I wouldn't give for that.

I am sorry, I have been very self-absorbed by this whole situation.

Don't worry. I understand. I probably would be acting just like you.

The Fathers, and Sister, have been very good, it's just I can't wrap my head around it.

Who can?

Thanks for the talk, Ryan.

You're very welcome.

We will keep praying for Delilah.

Trip and Shirley had brought the O'Doyles a very lovely vase of flowers – tiger lilies, Alice's favorite.

When they were ready to leave the demon became violent. She broke through her restraints and charged at Delilah at the door, grabbing Delilah's hair and pulling her to the floor. She was too fast for them.

YOUR TIME HAS ALMOST COME.

Ken ran to the door and sprinkled Holy Water on her.

IZGORILO.

Get her away from us.

I hoped you would have more compassion for Alice, Ken yelled.

Alice is still trapped inside there. She is not a wild animal.

That's exactly what she is.

Delilah was in shock – Ken shook her.

Delilah, it's over, snap out of it.

They ran out the door.

They restrained Alice once again and prayed.

Let's have a drink, Ryan; I really need one.

Me too.

Ryan, this situation would be funny if it wasn't so sad.

I know, Ken.

We are living together in the same house going through all this.

You love my Lizzy. Let's get that drink, Ken. I don't think we can wait any longer for the Exorcism.

I agree, we're breaking down; we both are taking pills and drinking alcohol in the morning.

They felt hopeless.

I am going to get the paper, Ken; it is the morning, remember.

Ryan went to the mail box; on the step there were two white doves. They flew away when they saw Ryan.

Ken, come quickly.

The doves were out of sight when Ken got to the door.

There were two doves on the steps; you missed it.

I don't get it? Ken asked.

Doves are at funerals as a sign of the afterlife. I never believed that before; I do now.

To me they're the sign of release. What do you think?

I hope you are right. Now we have something drink for!

Not just to escape, Ken added.

Father Seamus went for a walk. He loved feeding the birds; they made them feel at peace with the world. He startled two birds in a bush – they were doves.

It's a sign we are going to have deliverance; I must get back to the rectory.

He walked briskly.

Father Robert, you will not believe what happened! I startled two white doves in a bush. This is a sign from God, man.

That is very encouraging, Father Seamus.

It is time, man, for you to stop your medication.

Okay, here, I will give them to you for safekeeping.

Father Robert called Ryan.

Ryan, we have a sign.

So did I.

Doves, they both said.

Father Seamus startled them in a bush before they flew away.

They were on my steps.

This is the best thing we have had in a long time.

Please come to the house.

Father Robert and Father Seamus arrived at the house, and everyone was very excited.

Do you really believe it's a sign? asked Eileen and Elizabeth.

I see the sign of a deliverance. It's a sign also of rebirth.

Finally they had good news to tell one another.

I told Father Robert to stop taking the drug.

No, he needs to be weaned off them – it affects the heart.

Sorry, should have known better. That will have to do, Ryan. We will begin tonight. We both have been fasting again; this is the fourth day. We must go back to the Archdiocese to begin.

Father Seamus did all the talking to Archbishop McKean.

We have our sign, tis two doves. Ryan also saw the doves. Deliverance is upon us. Can we go ahead with the Exorcism?

Have you both done the fasting?

Yes, they both replied.

Begin the Exorcism.

CHAPTER SIX

THE EXORCISM

At the house the demon screamed: *IT'S TIME FOR THE PIT. DEBTS WILL BE REPAID.*

They knew it was the beginning, possibly the end of their Alice forever.

The phone rang.

Ken, get the phone; we won't be able to take another disappointment.

This is Ken.

Ken, we will begin, said Father Seamus; *we all need confession.*

Father Robert heard Ken's confession. It was the hardest. How can absolution be given to a man who will continue the same sin? He was not even Catholic or baptized – he confessed anyway. His confession was short, but he never mentioned loving a married woman. Father Robert expected as much. The others all were given absolution.

There's only the three of us who will be involved in the Exorcism.

Why? asked Elizabeth. *It's our daughter!*

That is exactly why; she may die, Elizabeth.

Okay, I do not want to remember her that way.

Neither did anyone else.

Sister Mary, Father Robert, and Father Seamus had a duty to do. They went up to Alice's room.

HAVE YOU COME TO REPAY YOUR DEBT?

Father Seamus gave no comment.

In the name of the Father, Son, and the Holy Spirit.

They all crossed themselves.

SHUT UP, YOU PIECE OF SHIT.

Lord have mercy on Alice Elizabeth O'Doyle, even when you know her as a sinner. Deliver her from the darkness she is in. Give me your name, demon.

NEVER!

Give me a name and depart from this innocent child!

SHE SUMMONSED ME.

Depart from this child, Alice Elizabeth O'Doyle. You will give me a name, and return to the depths of Hell.

YOU HAVE NO POWER TO CAST ME OUT.

God demands it. The Saints demand it. Jesus the only God demands it.

The window smashed, and hornets flew into the room.

Do not stop, Father Robert, Sister Mary.

The room became unbearably hot. Hornets went up Father Seamus's robe. The morphine bottle smashed against the door. Alice arched her back and touched her toes. The restraints let go; Alice levitated and latched to the wall. The demon let out a horrible shriek.

They watched Alice crawl up the wall.

You have no power to take her to the pit; only our Lord has the authority to pass judgment.

Everyone sprinkled her with Holy Water.

Help us Jesus Christ!

The closet door flew open. The tunnel of flames returned.

HELP ME, BROTHERS!

Sister Mary was dragged under the bed.

Return the Holy Sister.

In the room there was dead silence. Demons flew out of the flames, and all hell broke loose. Demons circled the bed.

Lord Jesus Christ, defeat the powers of these demonic creatures.

Sister Mary had a vision of the gas the chambers in Dachau. She had to witness women and children being gassed. She could not breathe. She was stripped completely naked and was being sent to the showers. Then she saw hundreds of Jews being burned alive. Children being thrown from windows. The sheer feeling of terror was so great she thought she would die of fright.

Father Robert had a vision of Idi Amin slaughtering hundreds of Ugandan people. He could feel their terror.

Father Seamus had a vision of Nero killing his mother.

They watched Russian Jews being gassed in a Russian gulag. Father Robert began to cry.

Don't show weakness, Father Robert; the demon will gain strength.

I AM TIMELESS. I CAN GO ON FOREVER.

Leave this child, cried Father Seamus.

HER SOUL IS DAMNED.

It rained rocks. The rocks banged down on them. The house was taking hard blows. All the lights in the house went out.

We need to get candles, Father Seamus.

Get them, Sister Mary.

Sister Mary had a hard time on the stairs; it felt like she was walking in quicksand. She began to float down the stairs.

In the name of Jesus let me down.

She began to be lowered onto the stairs.

Thank you, Jesus.

Downstairs there was light. Elizabeth handed her a large candle. She retrieved it and tried to get to the stairs.

We need more Holy Water, Father Seamus.

Father Seamus grabbed a vase from the hallway. He ran it under the bathroom sink and blessed it. Father Seamus and Sister Mary returned to the room. In the bedroom mirror three demons danced.

Sister Mary had a vision of Jesus hanging upside down on the cross. She dipped her hand in the vase and crossed herself.

Leave this child of God.

SHE IS MINE.

You have no Authority!

MY FATHER HAS GIVEN ME AUTHORITY.

There is only one true Father, Jesus Christ.

FUCK OFF, BITCH.

Seamus help me.

Ruler of darkness, go back to the pit which you came from.

NEVER.

Father Robert stepped forward.

Creature of evil, leave this godly child.

SHE CALLED ME, SHE BROKE RULES, AND THIS GIVES THE AUTHORITY.

God has authority.

WHERE IS YOUR GOD? HE DOES NOT THINK SHE IS WORTHY!

Every soul has worth; you are a liar.

Father Robert, I will take it from here.

Yes, Father Seamus.

I will banish you, demon; God demands it!

I WILL NEVER LEAVE, SHE IS WARM; WE STAY.

You are not staying in this child of God.

I HAVE CROSSED THE BARRIER TO FIND A HOST. YOU KNOW THE RULES, MAGGOT, IF I GET AN INVITATION, I HAVE THE RIGHT TO BE HERE.

God has revoked your invitation. Give me a name, demon!

The demon laughed.

God is stronger than you, demon; give me a name and leave.

STILL DRINKING, FATHER ROBERT.

Be gone, ancient ruler from hell.

A succubus showed up in the mirror. It put its hands through the mirror. Sister Mary felt an icy hand go down her back. Outside big torrents of rain came into the room.

Keep going, Sister Mary, Father Robert. Twister of truth, leave this innocent child.

THE SWINE IS MINE.

The innocent child is God's.

SHE IS NOT AN INNOCENT CHILD. SHE IS WORTHLESS SCUM, A PIECE OF PLANKTON.

You will give me a name, creature of darkness, and leave forever.

NAMES ARE FORBIDDEN IN THE PIT; MANY OLD FRIENDS WISH TO MEET HER.

Leave this godly child.

GOD THINKS SHE IS WORTHLESS!

Every soul has worth, Prince of Darkness.

Downstairs they had their own piece of Hell. All of Alice's tropical fish had died, and were floating to the top of the tank. They were having a vicious storm, and the fridge was floating in mid-air. Biggie Smalls was in the garage; he refused to enter the house. Out the front window on the lawn two green eyes were staring at them.

What is that, Ryan? Elizabeth pointed out the window.

I think it's a very big dog.

What's it want?

Right then the dog began to bark at the house, sounding very vicious. Biggie Smalls moaned loudly from the garage.

Mom, come see this dog.

Eileen went to the front window.

Jesus, Mary, and Joseph, what does it want?

I think he wants in the house, said Ryan.

That's not going to happen, Ryan.

I know, Eileen.

It's a very large dog, Ryan.

Yes, it's the color of his eyes that has me concerned, said Elizabeth; *they look like wolf eyes.*

You're right, bubble.

The dog had been barking all along.

Eileen, Lizzy, let's get away from the window.

They all backed away.

Back upstairs Father Seamus was trying to drive out the demon.

Noon day devil, leave this child.

The demon started to roar, shaking the room. Perfume bottles and jewelry began to crash at the door. A bottle of perfume exploded in mid-air.

SHE BELONGS TO MY FATHER!

She belongs to Christ.

FUCK YOU, MAGGOT; SHE BELONGS WITH THE WORMS.

Be quiet, said Sister Mary.

SHUT UP, YOU WHORE!

Sister Mary, do not listen to it. Father Robert's pain was returning.

YOU WANT YOUR PILLS, OLD MAN; I CAN MAKE YOU PAIN EVEN GREATER.

Father Robert doubled over from the pain. Sister Mary sprinkled Holy Water on Father Robert.

Fallen angel, he who has been cast out of heaven, leave the child!

I EXIST TO CAUSE TORMENT. I WILL CONTINUE TO TORMENT THIS CHILD.

You have no power over God's will.

Alice began to scream. Father Seamus doubled over in pain.

SEE, I DO HAVE THE POWER TO CONTINUE WITH THE ASSAULT.

Father Robert yelled, *Leave, you abomination of God.*

WHEN SHE IS ROTTING IN THE PIT, YOU WORTHLESS SCUM.

Father Robert had a great pain in his heart.

Jesus, please protect me.

We need a break, said Father Seamus.

Everybody was exhausted. Ryan was the first to enquire if they were done.

No, Ryan, we need more time, said Sister Mary.

Okay, we don't know what to expect. Each and every time it is different, Ryan.

I didn't know that, Sister Mary.

Yes, Ryan, each time is different, but always a war, which can become violent.

Violent?

Yes, Elizabeth. It's a age-old war, the war between good and evil, said Father Seamus.

Does evil ever win?

Not in the Exorcisms I have performed, Ryan.

That is very good to hear, Father Seamus.

Well, we should get back to it, said Father Seamus; *is everybody ready?*

Yes, Father Seamus.

Very good, let's proceed.

The foundation of the house began to shake.

Prepare yourself, Sister Mary, Father Robert.

Yes, Father Seamus.

They headed up the stairs. Alice was just sitting on the bed.

YOU PEOPLE SICKEN ME!

Shut up, demon.

SUCH A FOUL-MOUTHED SISTER.

Alice had a teddy bear collection. Her stuffed polar bear began to scream. Her Victorian dolls began to dance. Her musical jewelry box began to play a series of moaning sounds. Her curtains began to open and close. The room was covered in rats. A rat ran up from under her sheets and it ran up Alice's face. Alice grabbed the rat. She stuck out her tongue and her tongue caught the rat and she began to eat it. They could hear the tiny bones being crunched slowly. Father Robert gagged. She sucked the tail back like a string of spaghetti. After she ate it, she smiled. Rat blood and fur were caught between her teeth.

Sister Mary ran out of the room and into the bathroom to throw up. The demon just laughed.

You sickening demon, stop your foul behavior.

WHAT A SHOW I PROVIDE MY GUESTS.

Sister Mary returned to the room.

I'm sorry, Seamus, Robert.

It is not a problem, Mary.

Thank you, Seamus.

We forgot our jackets before coming back, I will get them.

Thank you, Sister Mary.

No problem, Robert.

The storm continued.

Here we go, Seamus, Robert, your coats.

Thank you again, Sister Mary.

Not only were they fighting for Alice's soul, the bedroom window was smashed in and they were fighting the elements. It was a bad thunderstorm. Baseball-sized balls of ice began to hail down and to fly around the room. Sister Mary was hit.

Stop it in the name Christ – it stopped. *Stop this show, and return to the depths of Hell. God commands it.*

Outside the lightning danced across the sky. The elements came down on them like a continuing assault.

God demands you to stop all of your tricks.

YOUR GOD'S NOT HERE!

You're a liar, cried Father Robert.

YOU'RE A FUCKING DRUNK; FATHER SEAMUS, YOUR PRIEST IS WEAK, TOO BAD FOR YOU.

Father Robert is a man of God. He is a good man. We will drive you out of this girl.

TRY! YOU WILL NOT. I WILL BE TAKING HER TO HELL. MY FATHER HAS PROMISED ME SHE IS MINE.

Our Lord will save her soul.

HOW IS CLARE? The demon howled with laughter.

Clare was Father Seamus's daughter. Father Seamus was weak when it came to the only woman he ever loved. Erin was his high school girlfriend. He decided after high school he was going to be a priest. It was a hard decision, and Erin was crushed.

Just before taking his vows, he slipped. That's when Clare was conceived. Father Seamus informed the church of his fall. He told the church if they still wanted him to be a priest, he must support the child and be involved in her life. The church was not happy, but agreed.

You leave my child out of this.

Sister Mary knew about Clare. Father Robert was shocked.

SHE CAN PAY FOR YOUR ACTIONS, PRIEST.

Father Seamus was truly scared for Clare.

You will be cast back to hell!

THERE ARE OTHERS, PRIEST.

Ryan came to the door.

Father Seamus, she needs to take her Seroquel.

Okay, please come into the room.

Ryan walked into the room. He did not know what to expect and was uneasy.

Ryan, please understand it is a process; we will have success.

I believe you, Father Seamus.

YOU WILL NOT WIN THIS WAR.

Give me a name and leave, demon!

NEVER!

Ryan gave Alice her shot.

Ryan, please leave now.

Yes, Father Robert.

YOU ARE NOT ALL POWERFUL.

Look at the cross, you cruel demon.

A loud scream came from the demon.

GET IT AWAY.

No, I will continue to harass you until you leave. You will find no refuge here.

Alice was emaciated. Everyone was terribly worried about her weight. It was hard to visualize her as Alice anymore. Ken came to see how things were going.

He had been gone for two days, to try to get his office in functioning order. He told his boss at St. Michael's he was taking a leave of absence. His boss was understanding but a little confused.

How is it going, you guys?

We don't really know, said Ryan. *I am still giving her the Seroquel.*

That's good; it's too hard on the system to stop cold turkey.

I know, Ken.

Elizabeth was very happy to see him, but she tried not to show it.

Can I see her?

No, Father Seamus still feels it is not a good idea for us to be too involved in the Exorcism.

Well I'm sure he has a good reason.

Let's hope it is over soon, Ken.

We just have to be patient, Elizabeth.

I'm happy you're back. Is your boss understanding?

Yes, he was. He is confused but I had a month of holidays I usually take in the fall. I think that's where he thought I was.

Ryan was his own boss, and Kelly understood, and tried to take on Ryan's patients as well as his own practice. He was getting burned out though.

The living room couch started to levitate. Every time something started to levitate everyone got worried. The couch slowly moved to the floor.

A terrible scream came from Alice's room.

Father Robert recited the Saint Michael's prayer. It seemed to cause the demon the greatest pain.

Leave, you Enemy of the human race. Your time is coming when you will be driven back to hell.

SHUT UP, YOU BITCH.

Sister Mary was unfazed by the demon's cruelty; she had heard it all before and more. She was a formidable woman.

They all began to pray for Alice's deliverance.

YOUR PRAYERS FALL ON DEAF EARS.

Return to Hell from which you came, shouted Father Seamus. *Give me a name, demon, and the time which you will depart.*

I WILL NEVER DEPART, YOU FAGGOT.

Jesus commands you to depart from this child. Jesus demands you leave.

MY FATHER DEMANDS I STAY. SHE IS SO WARM, WE STAY.

The room was incredibly cold, and the storm continued unabated. It sounded like the house was going to be torn apart. Downstairs the furniture kept levitating. The coffee table flew across the room and almost hit Eileen. Everyone was praying.

Eileen, are you alright?

I'm fine, Ryan. But my nerves are shot! Eileen was shaking, and couldn't stop.

Eileen, you need to take something to stop the shakes.

Ryan went and got her a Xanax.

I do not want to take it.

As a doctor, Eileen, I'm telling you to take it. I started Ryan on it; it is a necessary evil.

Okay, Ken, maybe I should just listen to you.

Please do, Eileen. It will calm you down.

Eileen took the Xanax. Upstairs the battle continued.

YOU ALL WILL PAY FOR YOUR PART IN THIS. YOU PRIESTS ARE GOING TO PAY THE MOST. YOUR NAME WILL BE REMEMBERED IN HELL.

Your threats do not scare me, demon.

THEY SHOULD, SEAMUS.

Christ will protect me; he always has.

NOT THIS TIME!

Father Seamus grabbed his stomach. Sharp, shooting pains were going through it. He sprinkled Holy Water on it, and the pain ceased.

You malevolent creature, your time is coming to an end.

I AM TIMELESS. I WILL ALWAYS HAVE A HOST. GACY WAS ALSO A PROTÉGÉ OF MINE. HE KNEW HOW TO HAVE FUN. ALL THOSE BOYS HE KILLED WERE HAND PICKED BY ME. OF COURSE HE HAD HIS OWN SKILLS.

Be quiet, you demon.

They continued their prayers, which caused the demon great pain.

SHUT UP, YOU BASTARDS. SPEAKING OF BAS-TARDS, FATHER ROBERT, WHAT DOES IT FEEL LIKE TO BE A BASTARD?

Father Robert's mom was only sixteen when she gave birth to Robert. He was often teased by bullies telling him he was a bastard.

SO HOW IS YOUR WHORE OF A MOTHER?

My mother is a saint; she is as wonderful as she always has been.

OH THAT'S RIGHT ,YOU ALWAYS WERE A FUCKING LITTLE MAMA'S BOY. CLARE IS A DAD-DY'S LITTLE GIRL. MY FRIENDS WOULD LOVE TO MEET CLARE; I WILL PASS THEM A MESSAGE.

This was not the first time Father Seamus's loved ones had been threatened, but its mention of Clare scared Father Seamus.

You cruel demon, be gone from this child.

IT WILL NOT BE SO EASY THIS TIME, PRIEST. LEGION STANDS BEHIND ME; WE WILL NOT GO.

They heard a girl quietly say in a low voice, *Please help me, Father.*

Alice, is that you?

As fast as it came it went.

Was that Alice's voice, Robert?

I think it was!

Let the child go, demon! Your pain will be greater for harming this innocent child.

IT MATTERS NOT TO ME, HER INNOCENCE, I DO NOT CARE. ROBBING THE INNOCENT IS WHAT I DO. TED BUNDY WAS ALSO A FRIEND OF MINE, AND STILL IS. NO REMORSE IS WHAT HE UNDERSTOOD MOST. MURDER WAS HIS WAY OF LIFE.

This upset Father Seamus and Sister Mary. They had always talked about where certain killers get their ideas and compulsions from. John Wayne Gacy had a terrible compulsion to rob the innocents and kill. At the end he said he was innocent of his crimes. No remorse!

You have used people to carry out your horrible crimes, said Father Seamus.

MOST OF THESE CRIMES THEY ENJOYED A GREAT DEAL. I WOULD WATCH THEIR CRIMES AND ENJOY MYSELF, UNTIL I GREW TIRED OF WATCHING THE SAME OLD STORY. I LIKE VARIETY IN MY CRIMES.

You enjoy this a great deal. You rob all life, said Sister Mary.

YES I DO, I AM A ROBBER OF LIVES.

RICHARD RAMIREZ TRULY LOVED BEING EVIL, NOW HE WAS A DISCIPLE. HE CARRIED OUT MY EVIL SO WELL. I INFORMED HIM OF WHERE THIS EVIL CAME FROM, AND HE LOVED IT. DAHMER WAS A DISAPPOINTMENT; HE WAS ALWAYS SWITCHING SIDES.

It is time for another rest, Father Robert, Sister Mary.

They needed to digest this evil, and they went

downstairs. They needed to figure out just how far a demon would go to rob innocents.

How is everything going, Father Seamus?

We can't continuously listen to evil, Ken. We need a reprieve for a while.

I think we all understand it. We took shifts to keep us sane.

That is what we need also, time away from the evil, Ryan.

We understand, Sister Mary.

Thank you for your understanding, Ryan.

Everyone was on the same page with their emotions.

What's next? asked Ryan.

We persevere with the fight until good wins.

This was the only option.

While they were talking a fire started in the fireplace. Eileen was facing the fireplace so she noticed it first. She could make out demon faces in the flames. The fireplace lit up, and faces of demons appeared. Everyone turned their attention to the fireplace. Nobody asked why it was happening anymore, just when it would happen.

This house has inhabited evil right to its core.

I know, Seamus, you are right, said Father Robert.

Mary and Ken concurred with the Fathers. Ryan, Elizabeth, and Eileen did not wish to look at their once happy home coming to this.

Father Seamus and Father Robert began to bless each room. Everyone went with the Fathers. They had plenty of opposition from the evil forces.

We will be in another battle; please understand this.

They knew Sister Mary was right. In the kitchen Ken had a steak knife thrown at him. In the living room Eileen was punched in the stomach by unseen hands.

In the downstairs bathroom all the taps were turned on to hot, and flooded the room. In the study, books went flying in everyone's direction. Out in the inside porch, flames came out of the lights. On the deck it rained rocks. They forgot the garage.

They went upstairs to start the blessing. Ryan was thrown down four steps and sprained his right hand. Elizabeth ran down to help Ryan and tripped on the last stair. Something was preventing them from even blessing the upstairs.

This is where we will get the most resistance; it is where Alice's room goes to.

Father Robert was correct. When they went into Ryan's and Elizabeth room, there were wasp nests everywhere. Father Seamus took the brunt of the attacks. He had stings everywhere on his body. In the main hallway, pictures fell off the wall. Sister Mary's rosary was grabbed from her hand. It floated to the ceiling and exploded. In the upstairs bathroom, all the taps exploded, covering everyone in hot water. In Eileen's sewing room, knitting needles were thrown at Ken, many hitting him. In the spare bedroom their cross on the dresser was turned upside down and floated in mid-air. They were blocked from coming into Alice's room. The door was locked.

Father Seamus sprinkled Holy Water on it, and the door flew open. Alice's bed was blocked by dark hooded figures. They turned around and looked at them; they were hideously evil. They then turned around and began to pray over Alice. Everyone knew the dark demonic creatures were praying to the evil in Alice.

Father Seamus had a small cross that was blessed by

Padre Pio. He knew he would need the holy object in battle. The figures disappeared. They blessed Alice with Holy Water.

IZGORILO, STAY AWAY FROM THIS CHILD.

She is not your child! screamed Sister Mary.

SHE IS MY CHILD NOW!

You have possessed her soul, she is not yours! shouted Father Robert.

An image of Padre Pio appeared, and they could finally reach Alice.

Who is that?

It is a priest named Padre Pio; he performed many Exorcisms. He also has appeared during many successful Exorcisms. Robert, this is a blessing in our favor.

Sister Mary started with the Lord's Prayer; Father Robert and Father Seamus joined in.

Holy Father, relieve Alice Elizabeth O'Doyle from the wickedness she endures. Holy Mother of God, grant her deliverance from the powers of evil. Defeat this demonic creature inside her, and this house of its presence.

The Holy Mother appeared in the mirror. It was another blessing in their favor; it showed them God could see Alice's suffering. They never asked why; they knew there was a reason from God. In each Exorcism time was irrelevant.

The cross Father Robert held in his hand began to burn him. He ran to the bathroom and ran it under the tap. They seemed to have interference after a blessing; it was very tiring. Father Robert quickly returned to the Exorcism.

We are tiring of you, demon.

FATHER ROBERT, I AM NOT TIRING OF YOU, I CAN GO ON AND ON. I'M NEVER TIRED BY MY EVIL DEEDS. IN THESE TIMES MANY PEOPLE DELIGHT IN BEING EVIL. RIGHT TO THE VERY END. KEVIN WAS WORKING HIS EVIL. A FOOL PROVIDED A GREAT TIME FOR OUR WORK. HE THOUGHT HE WAS DOING GOOD. WE ALWAYS WERE WORKING TOGETHER, HE AND I. WE WERE ABLE IN A PRISON WITH SECURITY AND GUARDS TO GET OUR HANDS AROUND HIS NECK. IT WAS SHEER DELIGHT. I EVEN LIKE THE ONES IN PRISON WHO FIND GOD. I AM STILL IN THEIR MINDS! LET FREE THEY ALWAYS COME BACK TO ME.

HOW I ENJOY WATCHING THEIR WORK. THEY ARE ALL FOOLS OF COURSE TO THINK AT THE LAST MINUTE I WILL PROTECT THEM. I ONLY WAIT UNTIL THEY ROT IN HELL. THEY ALL RETURN HOME TO HELL, TO CONTINUE TOR-TURING LOST SOULS.

MANY OF MY PROTÉGÉS CONTINUE TO TELL THE MASSES OF SOCIETY THEY WILL KILL AGAIN. SOME SAY THEY WILL NOT KILL AGAIN. THESE FOOLS BELIEVE THEIR OWN LIES. THEY WILL CONTINUE TO ROB, AND MURDER TILL THE END. THEY ALL COME TO LEGION IN THE END. OF COURSE MANY WOMEN COME TO ME. MANY PEOPLE BELIEVE WANDA WAS ONLY KILLING IN SELF DEFENCE. I KNOW THE TRUTH; I PUT IT THERE. SHE ALREADY HAD A GREAT URGE TO ATTACK SOCIETY. I GAVE HER THE MEANS.

LISA WAS ONE HELL OF A WOMAN. HER LUST LED HER TO MY DOOR. SHE LOVED TO WATCH HER LOVER MURDER; IT TURNED HER ON. SHE OF COURSE IN THE END DID WHAT A LOT OF THEM DO, BLAME THEIR LOVER. WE KNOW THE REAL TRUTH.

ALAN FOUND THE RIGHT BABE IN CONNIE. HE HAD THE HOTS FOR A VICTIM. SHE MUTI-LATED AND TORTURED THE BITCH.

DENISE WAS A WOMAN IN NEED OF A CHILD. SHE KILLED HER FRIEND, CUT THE CHILD RIGHT OUT OF HER STOMACH WHILE SHE WATCHED. I KNOW; WE PLOTTED IT TOGETHER. I STILL LISTEN TO THE CRAZY BITCH.

KELLY AWAYS KNEW WHAT SHE LIKED. SHE WORE A PENTAGRAM AROUND HER NECK, HAD HER BOYFRIEND DO HER ART WORK.

TINA AND FAMILY LOVED MONEY, AND DEATH. HIGH ON THEIR OWN SUPPLY, THEY BUTCHERED A MAN FOR FUN.

A NICE CATHOLIC GIRL FROM ALBERTA, CANADA, KILLED HER FAMILY TO KEEP WEARING MY ATTIRE.

ANOTHER NICE CATHOLIC GIRL FROM CANADA KILLED HER SISTER TO CONTINUE TO CARRY OUT MURDER WITH HER FIANCÉ. LEGION HAS CLAIMED SOME OF THE SOULS ALREADY. OTHER WE WATCH CLOSELY AND WAIT FOR THEIR SOULS.

Enough, you demon, I do not want to hear any more of your

cruelty, said Father Seamus. *You have been very busy over the years.*

THEY SAY EVIL LIES IN THE HEARTS OF MAN, WHICH IS TRUE. I DO NOT PUT THE EVIL THERE. IT WAS ALWAYS WAS THERE. TO ME IT'S LIKE A DRY BUSH AND SOMEONE THROWS A LIT CIG-ARETTE INTO IT. THEN THERE'S A FOREST FIRE. I AM OF COURSE THE LIT CIGARETTE; WHAT A FIRE!

The Demon began to laugh.

DO YOU KNOW HOW MUCH I LOVE TO WATCH MOTHERS WHO KILL THEIR CHILDREN? NANCY KILLED NINE OF HER KIDS FOR ATTENTION. DIANNE SHOOTS HER CHILDREN BECAUSE HER LOVER WANTS NO CHILDREN. SUSAN DROWNS HERS KIDS BECAUSE HER LOVER WANTS NO KIDS. THEY WILL ALL RETURN TO LEGION.

The room went ice cold. The demon became very silent. The closet opened up, and they could see the tunnel of fire. They could see armies of demons marching in the tunnel up to the room. Father Seamus, Father Robert, and Sister Mary watched in horror.

This is not anything I have seen before, said Father Seamus.

I told you he was high in Satan's Court, replied Sister Mary.

Father Robert was silent. He grabbed the vase of Holy Water and threw it into the tunnel. The tunnel disappeared.

Thank you, Father Robert.

You're welcome, Sister Mary.

That was very fast thinking, said Father Seamus.

Downstairs a roar could be heard.

What in God's name is going on down there?

They went running downstairs. Looking out of the fireplace was the flaming face of a lion.

What's going on? asked Father Seamus.

I do not know, said Ryan.

It is the Noon Day Devil, said Sister Mary.

Of course, Sister Mary. Go get some more water, Father Robert, and bless it quickly.

They thought it would likely light the house on fire, and they waited for Father Robert. He came back, and brought a pot full on Holy Water and threw it into the flames. The fire decreased but did not go out completely; they could still see a lion face imprinted on the back of the fireplace.

What was that?

I do believe it is a sign from the demon, that he's very powerful like Sister Mary said, replied Father Seamus.

What does it want with my daughter?

I do not know, Elizabeth.

I am very tired, everyone, said Father Robert.

I believe we all should rest, said Sister Mary.

We will rest in shifts, Father Robert, Sister Mary. I will work the first shift.

Thank you, Seamus.

Father Seamus returned to Alice's room.

ALL ALONE, PADDY?

I don't care, demon!

YOU SHOULD, PADDY. I HAVE SIXTY LEGIONS BEHIND ME.

I have Christ. He is more powerful than your legions!
WE WILL SEE, PADDY.
What do you want with this girl?
THAT'S A SECRET, the demon laughed.

Father Robert and Sister Mary went for a rest. Sister Mary dreamed she saw a woman in Africa, a missionary, holding an African little boy. She seemed to be comforting this little boy. She then saw her giving the boy a St. Michael's medallion. She was not wearing a habit, but Sister Mary knew she was a nun. She went to walk over and meet this nun, as she got closer she realized it was Alice. *Hello, Alice. Hello, Sister Mary.* Then she woke up.

She needed to talk to Father Seamus, and went up to see him.

Mary, what are you doing up?
Alice is going to be a nun.
What do you mean?
I saw it in my dream. I dreamt I saw her in Africa, helping the poor.
My God, that's why this demon has possessed her. She is going to be very important to the church.
I think so, Father.

Alice was asleep, thank the Lord. She woke up as soon as Sister Mary and Father Seamus were talking in the room.

SHE WILL NEVER BECOME A NUN, YOU SWINES. SHE WILL ROT IN HELL BEORE THAT EVER HAPPENS.
You are a liar, demon.
MY LEGION WILL WIN THIS TIME.

Alice began to levitate. She went to the ceiling and

hung upside down. As Sister Mary and Father Seamus began to recite the Lord's Prayer, she slowly lowered.

Destructor of souls, give me a name.

SHE WILL ROT IN HELL BEFORE THAT HAPPENS.

You have no authority over her damnation.

WE'LL SEE, WE'LL SEE, PRIEST.

Leave this innocent girl. Your pain in Hell will be greater for your actions.

They restrained Alice once more.

Downstairs the doorbell rang.

I'll get it!

Okay, Ken.

Who would be calling at this time in the night, Ken?

I don't know, Eileen; I'll see.

Hello, how can I help you?

The first thing Ken noticed was this man's attire; he was dressed in a black robe.

My name is Alistair; I was wondering if you would like to know the way of the Anti-Christ.

What?

The Anti-Christ, would you like to know how to reach the path of eternal wisdom?

Get the fuck out of here, you freak!

Can I see the girl? I have been told about her.

I told you get the fuck off this porch, and leave.

Not before we see the girl.

He pushed Ken to get in the door.

One thing about Ken, he worked out in the gym, every day. He grabbed the man and put him in a head-lock. Other men came from behind the bush. They tried to get past Ken.

What's wrong, Ken?

Ryan, get the gun.

Ryan ran to his room. The others ran up the stairs.

Ryan had retrieved the gun. The other men were heading for Alice's room.

Stop right there, before I put a bullet in your heads.

We will leave, no need for the gun. We just wanted to see the girl.

Get the fuck out of my house.

Okay, okay, we're leaving, man.

Ken still had Alistair in a headlock; he let him go as soon as the others left the house.

Leave, you scum.

Alistair and the men left the house.

What in hell was that all about, Ken?

I have no idea, Elizabeth.

Everyone was shook up.

How did they know, Ryan?

I don't know, Ken.

What is happening? asked Eileen.

Some crazies, I don't know.

How did they know to come to our house, Ken?

Should we call the police, Ryan?

We would have to explain why we have our daughter tied up, Lizzy. There is no way even with us being doctors, Lizzy.

You're right, said Eileen. *Let's just leave it.*

If they come back, Lizzy, we take care of it then.

Father Robert went downstairs. *What's happening?*

Some crazies came to the door, I think they were Satanists, wanted to see Alice, said Ryan.

Good God, how did they know?

We don't know, and probably better if we just leave it. If they come back we will deal with it then.

Okay, Ryan, you're the head of the house.

How's Alice?

The same, Ryan, but we will have success.

We have to believe that, Father Robert.

Father Robert went back upstairs.

WHAT HAPPENED TO MY FRIENDS, PRIEST?

You sent for them, didn't you?

YES, THEY ARE MY DISCIPLES.

What are you talking about?

Some Satanists came to the door, wanted to see Alice, Seamus.

I HAVE FRIENDS, YOU SEE, PEOPLE WHO WANT TO SEE SUCCESS.

You are a foul creature, said Sister Mary.

I KNOW.

Great orbs of dark were circling the bed, followed by orbs of light. The dark orbs disappeared.

I think the orbs of lights were angels; the orbs of black were demons.

I think you're right, Seamus, said Sister Mary.

Let's continue, Father Robert.

They started with the Lord's Prayer, and blessed Alice.

IZGORILO.

You have been disobedient with the Lord, banished from Heaven, to the depths of Hell. Give your name and the time of your departure.

FUCK YOU, PRIEST.

Ancient creature from hell, Christ demands you leave.

I COMMAND SIXTY LEGIONS; YOU CAN NOT BANISH ME, PRIEST.

Your Legions do not have power over Christ. In the name of Jesus Christ the Lord I banish you back to hell, demon.

Father Seamus grabbed the cross Padre Pio blessed and placed it on Alice's forehead.

IZGORILO, PRICK, GET THAT AWAY!

No, you ancient serpent, leave this child.

The closet door opened again, and black orbs flew out.

Oh angels of the Lord, banish these demonic creatures.

White orbs appeared; the dark orbs disappeared.

Thank you, Jesus, said Father Robert. *You are not so powerful, demon.*

We must continue, Father Robert, said Father Seamus. *Diabolical demon, go back to the depths of Hell.*

A black-hooded form appeared in the corner of the room. Father Robert was the first to notice. They could see no face when it turned towards them. Father Robert sprinkled it with Holy Water, and it disappeared. The black orbs reappeared; they were gathering into one giant ball. They sprinkled Holy Water on the orb, but it remained and headed towards Father Seamus and Alice.

More Holy Water, Father Robert.

Father Robert sprinkled it with Holy Water and it disappeared. Everyone thanked Jesus.

Ancient serpent, depart from this child of God.

A shining white light came from the window and shone towards Alice. Alice gasped.

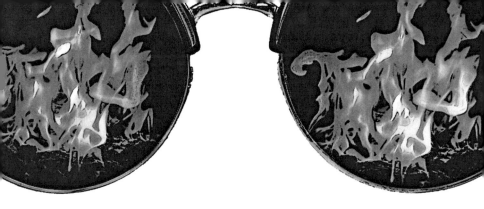

CHAPTER SEVEN

DELIVERANCE

A commanding voice came from the Light: ***Depart from my child, ABIGOR.***

A winged horse came out of Alice, then disappeared.

Out of the Light came another command: ***Continue the path I have chosen for each of you!***

Everyone wept.

Thank you, Jesus, cried Father Robert.

Alice gasped. Her face was surrounded by a white light.

Alice, is that you?

Yes, Father Robert, why are you here?

You've been sick; we came to pray for you. Do you remember anything, Alice?

I remember a dark tunnel. Why is that?

It must have been your fever, said Father Seamus.

Who are you?

My name is Father Seamus; this is Sister Mary.

Hello, Father Seamus; hello, Sister Mary. Thank you for your prayers.

You're most welcome, said Father Seamus and Sister Mary. Why am I tied up?

You were very violent with your fever.

Please untie me.

Of course, said Father Robert.

They untied her restraints. Alice got out of bed and looked in the mirror.

What happened to me?

All you need to know is you hurt yourself. It was the fever, said Sister Mary. You were hurting yourself again; that's why we had you restrained.

My God, I'm hideous!

It can all be fixed; it will take some time, said Father Seamus.

Where are my parents?

We will get them for you.

Thank you, Sister Mary.

Father Robert, go get them.

Yes, Father Seamus.

Father Robert went downstairs.

It is finished. She would like to see her family.

May I go?

I don't see why not, you are part of my family, Ken.

Thank you, Ryan.

Is it really over? said Eileen.

Yes, like I said, it is finished, your daughter was delivered by the hand of God. You must all go to church and repay the Lord. I have a baptism next week; please bring Alice. It is a rebaptism of all, anyone who has been baptized.

I want to be baptized, said Ken.

You will need to convert, and go to Bible class. You will need a Catholic sponsor.

I will be your sponsor, said Eileen.

Thank you, Eileen.

Let's go upstairs.

They entered Alice's room.

Mom, Dad, I look hideous.

What is Ken doing here?

I am here to help.

Thank you, Ken.

We will fix your hair and teeth, don't worry, honey.

How can I not worry; I have broken teeth and chopped hair.

We are just so happy you're well again, said Ryan. *You had a violent fever.*

Yes, you hurt yourself; we had to restrain you, said Elizabeth.

I know, Mom.

Be very thankful to God you're well.

Okay, Granma.

Let's all pray, said Eileen.

Everyone said the Lord's Prayer, including Ken.

We are so grateful, Lord, said Ken, *we give you thanks.*

Ken, aren't you an atheist?

Not anymore, Alice, I am a true believer.

He is converting to our faith, said Eileen.

No way!

Yes way, said Ken.

I still don't know how a fever could cause all this to happen to me?

Like your parents said, it was a bad, violent fever, said Father Robert.

What date is it?

It's November the second.

I was sick for that long.

Yes, honey, you were, said Ryan.

Do you feel good enough to go downstairs?

I need to take a shower first, Mom.

Okay, sweetheart. We'll meet you downstairs.

The shower was glorious. Alice came down to kitchen to to find out what really happened.

So guys, tell me what happened! Don't skip any information – I know you are lying.

You were possessed by a demon, Alice.

What?

It was the Ouija board you and Delilah were playing with.

I'll give you some advice, Alice. You were touched by the hand of God; not a lot of people have been so lucky. It is a miracle. A white Light shone down upon you and we believe it was the light of Christ. Out of the Light came a command for the demon inside you to leave. We can only assume it was St. Michael's voice, Father Robert explained.

MY GOD, said Eileen.

Yes, we are blessed, especially Alice.

Thank you so much, Fathers, Sister, said Ryan and Elizabeth.

Like you said, a true miracle.

Yes indeed, Ken.

Alice went upstairs to absorb the information. She came back downstairs in a pair of her skinny jeans and a Courtney Love t-shirt; she was drowning in them.

My clothes don't fit – I've lost a ton of weight!

We will get you all new ones, said Ryan.

Mom, I'm starving!

Tacos, babe?

Yeah, like three.

Everyone please have a seat in the living room. I will make some food.

We should be going, said Father Seamus.

I insist, said Elizabeth, *please stay. I know everybody is starving.*

This is a celebration. It won't seem right if you're not here, said Ryan.

We will stay, said Sister Mary.

We will go to the Archdiocese tomorrow, said Father Seamus.

Thank you, said Ken.

Everyone had a great meal. Alice ate, as predicted, three tacos.

Where's my cell phone, Mom? I couldn't find it in my room; I want to phone Delilah.

Elizabeth gasped. *Alice, when you were sick, Delilah came to visit. You were very cruel to her.*

Why?

It was like we've said, you were possessed by a demon.

What did I say to her? I want to know!

It's not important. I'll call Shirley first to tell her you're not sick anymore.

Okay, Mom, but I don't know why you have to call, when I can just call Delilah.

It's better this way.

Elizabeth went to make the call.

Hello, Shirley, it's Elizabeth.

Hello, Elizabeth, sorry how we left things; we didn't know how to react.

Everything is fine, Shirley. We have had a miracle; Alice is fine. Oh my God, she's Alice again.

Yes, thank the Lord.

Alice wants to talk to Delilah; she remembers nothing. Please talk to Delilah, we told Alice she was possessed by a demon. We told her she was cruel to Delilah. Just tell Delilah not to say anything.

I will, thank you for your understanding, Elizabeth; I know I wasn't there for you.

Everything is forgiven, Shirley.

Shirley told Delilah the story.

Mom, I don't care. Linda is my best friend now.

How can you be so cruel?

Just leave it, Mom.

Well, she is going to call you.

Well, I'm not going to answer!

What in God's name is wrong with you?

Hey, Mom it's the new me. I'm not your goody two shoes daughter anymore.

Delilah's phone rang.

If that's Alice calling, Delilah, pick the phone up, or you lose your car.

Hello.

Hi Di, it's me.

Hi Alice.

I'm sorry; I hear I was cruel to you when I was sick.

Yeah, whatever, Alice.

Di, what's wrong with you? I don't even remember what I did.

Yeah, okay, talk to you later.

Alice hung up the phone and cried. *Alice what's wrong?*

I talked to Delilah; she hates me!

She will come around; don't worry about it.

Don't worry about it? We are talking about an eleven-year friendship, Mom.

I know, sweetheart; give her some time.

If she knows I was sick, why would she be mad?

I don't know, said Eileen. *Just be happy with the fact that you are well.*

Well, that's fine. If she has no compassion, I don't want her as a friend.

That's very true. A true friend would understand, said Eileen.

Ryan walked back into the kitchen.

Mom, Dad, when can I get my teeth fixed?

On Friday, honey, Dr. Stone will see you then.

Great, they feel so disgusting. I guess I'm going to have short hair for a while.

Sweetheart, I will get in touch with Donna today, see if she can take you tomorrow.

Okay, Mom.

Don't you feel tired, luv?

No, Granma, I don't. I feel great!

That's wonderful, luv.

Well, we should leave now, said Father Robert. *We need rest.*

Of course, said Ryan, *we don't know how to repay you.*

You could donate to the Christmas for Everyone Foundation at the church, Ryan. The Foundation had a problem reaching its goal last year.

Will twenty thousand be enough?

More than enough; you're going to make a lot of families very happy this year.

Mom, Granma, when the stores open, can we go shopping?

Of course, but don't you want to rest a bit?

It feels like I've been resting for years; I am not tired.

Well if it's okay with everyone, we really must go now. Of course, Fathers, Sister.

I will come back tomorrow to check in on Alice, said Father Robert.

That would be great, said Elizabeth.

Well I'm going to sleep for a couple of hours before going in to see Kelly, said Ryan.

Well, I'm not sleepy, said Ken, *those tacos gave me a boost of energy. Can I hang here for a bit?*

Of course, I'll make coffee, Ken, said Elizabeth.

Good night, everyone, said Ryan.

Good night.

Well let's look at the flyers, see what's up in the fashion world, guys, said Eileen.

Sounds good, Granma.

Anything you want will be fine by me, said Elizabeth.

Great, Mom, new shoes too, Mom?

Sure!

Ken would like to come, said Alice.

Sounds like a blast.

Shopping with the girls sounds good to you? laughed Eileen.

I really do like shopping; it's one of my little secrets, Eileen.

Well, can't argue with that.

Everyone waited for the stores to open.

Back at the Shipleys, things were very tense. It was six in the morning and they could hear Delilah's stereo playing Iron Maiden.

What a ruckus, and it is so early in the morning, said Trip.

I know, said Shirley.

Who called so early?

Elizabeth, Alice is well again.
That's fantastic.
She doesn't remember a thing.
Well, that's just great news.
Trip, what do you think is wrong with Delilah? She has always been such a good girl now she's – I just don't know.
Well I'm going to tell her to turn down the music down! Delilah, turn down your music!
What?
Your music. TURN IT DOWN!
Whatever!
She turned down her music slightly.
Down, Delilah! What's the matter with you, Delilah?
Nothing, quit asking me that.
Well, you have gone from a straight "A" student to a hooligan.
I like the new me, Dad.
We don't! Get ready for school.
Delilah despised her parents. If they ever saw her boyfriend Ivan, they would freak out completely. It was cool with Ivan that he didn't have to meet her parents.
Well, only two hours, then off to Ivan's. I don't care if they find out I didn't go to school. It's Ivan's day off today. I want to spend quality time with him.
Ivan played in a house band at the Kabana; he was twenty three.
Well, I'll see you guys later.
Please drive safe, Delilah.
Where are you going? It's only six-thirty.
To Linda's to hang out.
Linda lived on her own. Delilah arrived at seven.
What's up, girlfriend? said Linda.

Parents driving me crazy, I talked to Alice.
Really?
Really!
Really! Is she still possessed?
They both laughed – secretly Delilah was still freaked out over the whole situation.
Let's get high, girlfriend, said Linda. *Have you done drugs, Delilah?*
No I haven't.
So you never shot Fentanyl?
What's Fentanyl?
It's like heroin.
Delilah was scared but did not want to show it.
Sure! I get it from Ian at the club.
Cool! I need to find a vein first.
Linda tied her off, and injected.
The world began to spin.
Holy crap, Linda!
Yeah, enjoy the trip, girl.
Delilah passed out. She was falling down a black tunnel. As she was falling she could feel cold hands touching her. She landed by a bog. She saw two hideous creatures; she could tell they were talking about her. They began to argue. Then one of the creatures was on top of her.
I have been waiting for you, Delilah, then she woke up.
Holy shit, Delilah tried to sit up but couldn't. *Help me sit up, Linda!*
Don't freak out, Delilah.
I was falling down a black tunnel and there were these awful creatures; they were very scary!

It's just part of the trip, it gets better.

I hope so.

You were just hallucinating, I have a couple of times myself.

Oh, well, I'm supposed to be going to Ivan's today.

Call him and tell him to drop by, but make sure he's got some weed.

Hey babe, what's up?

Why are you calling so early, ya stupid bitch?

What?

It's like seven-twenty in the morning.

I just shot some Fentanyl with Linda, thought you would like to join us.

I'll be over in an hour!

See ya in a bit, foxy.

Ivan's coming over in an hour, Linda.

Is he going to bring some weed?

Well, he always does.

Good.

Ivan was there in forty-five minutes.

What's up, foxy?

Just waiting for you.

Hey, Linda, can I have some?

Sure!

Did you bring weed?

Always.

Ivan had shot up quite a bit. He just sat back and enjoyed the ride.

This is top product, where did you get it?

From Ian, he always scores for me.

What would your parents be saying now, foxy?

Who cares, I'm moving in with Linda soon, then they will have no say in what I do.

How can you afford it, foxy?

I have a trust fund; my granma set it up. It's set up so at sixteen I can start taking money out.

Like how much money, foxy?

Two hundred thousand.

Holy crap, said Linda.

I've already got in touch with David Fallows, my granma's lawyer. I will be getting ten grand at the end of the week. It's set up for a one-time payment of up to ten grand, and I'm taking it. I'll buy you a new guitar, Ivan.

That's so cool, foxy.

Well you can score next, rich BFF.

No problem, when I'm not so high we'll go to the cash machine. I can take some money off my credit card, my dad pays it anyways.

It's great having a rich girlfriend, said Ivan.

Delilah ordered some pizza and beer from Rocky's Pizza.

Here's fifty, Ivan; you'll have to pay for it.

Can I keep the change?

Sure, no problem.

Ivan was already thinking of a way to get money out of Delilah; this was his chance.

When can I get my new guitar?

Whenever you want, you just need to ask.

Okay, I'm asking.

We'll go tomorrow.

Sure and maybe some real quality weed.

No problem.

Can you buy me some new clothes, Delilah?
No problem.
Great, we'll go to Janis's, they have top-of-the-line clothes. That bitch who works there always gives me dirty looks whenever I go there.
Well I have an account with them, my dad can pay for it.

Linda was also looking for ways to spend Delilah's money. Who would have predicted she and Delilah would even become friends? Delilah used to be a little square. She was glad Alice got sick; that's why they became friends.

Who wants another hit? Delilah, your turn.

Delilah didn't really want another hit but she did not want to look bad.

Ivan and Linda had known each other for at least two years before they met Delilah. Delilah had no idea; they both wanted to keep it that way.

CHAPTER EIGHT

LINDA

Linda Banks never thought she would be friends with Delilah Shipley. She always thought the rich kids stuck together. Well, they usually did. When Alice got sick, she made her move. Linda's mom made good money – well, she was a stripper. Her mom spent all her money on drugs and guys. Linda had been living on her own since she was sixteen – Linda was eighteen. Linda's boyfriend Jamal paid her rent, and gave her money. Jamal was twenty-three. Linda didn't ever ask where he got money; she didn't care where it came from. Jamal was married with two kids, but he was usually over at Linda's.

What a mark, said Ivan to Linda.

No doubt, man.

Delilah had passed out.

Well, I think we both are getting a great deal.

Yeah, I know, Ivan.

She is just so fucking naïve.

Let's keep it that way, Ivan.

Ivan and Linda sat around and ate pizza and got high.

Jamal showed up at noon.

What's with her, Linda?

Oh, she passed out.

What are we doing today?

Fentanyl and weed, man.

How's it going, Ivan?

Great.

She can't hold her drugs or what?

No, she is very new at it, sweetie.

Well, I'm going to get high, darling.

Go for it, sweetie.

Jamal got high.

Let's put her in your room, darling.

Sure, help us, Ivan.

No problem.

They laid her out on Linda's bed.

Well let's party, guys.

Where did you meet her, Linda?

School couple of months ago. She is really rich, she is getting ten thousand at the end of the week, can you believe it?

What!

She has like two hundred thousand in trust from her grandmother. Her dad owns a Porsche dealership. She drives a 2012 Porsche.

Right on, I can work some angles with her, darling.

So can we, said Ivan.

I am going to ask her to get me a Porsche. Her dad must be loaded.

Cool, darling; I'll have a great time driving it.

Whatever you want, babe.

What am I going to get? I'm like her boyfriend.

Sky's the limit, Ivan, laughed Linda. *She's taking me to Janis's tomorrow. I'm going to get a whole new wardrobe.*

Linda always wanted to be rich, and Delilah wanted to be friends with Linda. She pretty much would do anything she asked.

Do ya think she's okay, guys?

She's fine, Ivan, said Jamal. *She's just in la-la world.*

Let's go check on her, said Linda.

Sure, I'll go, no problem, said Ivan. Ivan put a mirror up to her mouth – *Still breathing, she'll be fine. She's just passed out.*

I'm hungry; let's order Chinese.

I still have thirty dollars left from Delilah, said Ivan. *It's on me, guys! I'll go pick it up; I'll take the Porsche. Where's the keys?*

Her purse is on the counter, grab it.

Ivan went into Delilah's purse and found her keys and wallet.

Well, what do we have here? Holy shit, she has five hundred dollars! Want a hundred, Jamal?

Sure.

Can I have a hundred, Ivan?

No can do, Linda, you already have a sugar daddy.

I give you mine, darling.

Thank you, Jamal.

Here's two hundred, darling, because you're so hot.

Thanks, sugar daddy.

You can thank me later.

I want to drive, Ivan.

No problem, Jamal.

Let's put some miles on this baby.

Go for it, Jamal.

I always forget how nasty Linda can be.

I got to go to the club after we've got the food.

Why, Ivan?

Score, man, this kind of money I'll get some crack.

Sounds good to me, dude.

As soon as they got back to the house, Linda asked, *What took you so long?*

Went for a little spin, got some smoke and crack, here's the food.

Who needs food when there's crack?

You're a drug hog, Linda.

Always has been since I've known her, Ivan.

Then we will hit some clubs with our cash, they all laughed.

What a dumb bitch, eh?

Sure is darling, and she's moving in! I will find more ways to cash in on the bitch.

Do you like her, Linda?

Do you, Ivan?

There is going to be some good times, darling.

What are you guys doing? Delilah came in and asked.

Nothing, sweetie, just went to get some food.

Want some?

No, I feel kind of nauseated.

It's just the drug, kiddo; it happens the first couple of times, said Linda. *This is Jamal, Delilah.*

Hi, nice to meet you, Jamal, my hair's probably a mess. I'm going to freshen up in the bathroom.

Sure, BFF, take your time.

When Delilah left they all cracked up. Delilah had no idea she was being used. The trick was to get Delilah hooked; then she would be dependent on Linda.

What time is it, Linda?

It's early; it's eight.

Eight in the evening?

Yeah, why?

I've got to get going. My dad will blow a fuse, I never came home after school.

Just stay here, who cares, Delilah! Or are you still a little baby?

No! I'll call home though so they don't think I was kidnapped. Hello, Mom.

Where the hell are you? We were going to phone the police!

Relax, Mom, I'm at Linda's; I'm staying the night here.

Like hell you are, Delilah!

Mom, I am sixteen years old, old enough to make my own decisions.

Delilah hung up and turned off her phone.

There, I told the bitch, is there any more Fentanyl?

Yeah, sure, BFF, let me tie you off. Linda found a vein and injected.

Delilah was out again.

Like candy from a baby, watch and learn, guys. This is so good; I am the undoing of the stuck-up bitch.

That's what I like about you darling, so nasty!

I can't think of anything more exciting, Jamal.

Linda, Ivan, and Jamal hit some clubs. They say evil lies in heart of man; well sometimes it's a woman.

I wonder what the limits on her credit cards are?

Do not know, darling?

I know her MasterCard PIN; I watched her all last week when we were shopping.

Just use it till it gets rejected, Linda.

Good thinking, Ivan.

I be shopping myself, said Ivan.

That makes three of us, guys.

We'll go to the mall; it's open to midnight.

She'll be out till midnight.

We have to be back by midnight. I'll make sure I give her another shot, then we'll have four hours at least to hit some more clubs.

Sounds good, darling.

Let's see if I remember it, yeah, twenty eight, twenty five.

Let's see if it works.

Linda took a two thousand dollar cash advance.

Hope and cross your fingers, guys.

The machine dispensed the money.

Bingo, let's check the receipt.

Wow, twenty-five thousand dollar limit, hell, mall.

I'm going to keep the two thousand, and use the card at the mall.

Whatever you want, darling.

I have a big appetite for cash, said Ivan.

I was never going to try it myself, but great idea, Linda baby.

You have not called me that in years, sweetie.

Jamal was getting jealous.

Remember when you were my girl, Linda?

Of course, sweetie!

Cool it, guys, I have had enough.

You're married with two kids!

Three, darling, one more on the way.

What? Linda was going to cry. *You promised me you were going to get a divorce!*

Well, plans change, that's my business, darling. I want a couple more with Denise; she knows about you, babe, it's cool.

It's not cool with me!

So I'll just replace you with another if you can't handle it.

Linda shut up; she knew Jamal would do it.

I want a two carat diamond then!

No problem, we got the funds now. Let's shop!

They went to Max's Diamonds.

How many carats is that one?

Two point five carats, Ma'am.

How much is that?

It's a great quality diamond, Ma'am.

How much!

Seventy five hundred.

Let me see if it fits, I'm good for the cash.

Linda opened up Delilah's wallet, and grabbed her card.

Try it on, Ma'am.

Don't mind if I do. It fits perfectly, I'll take it.

Linda gave the salesman Delilah's card.

Anything else?

Let me find out. Guys do you want to pick up a chain?

Sure, said Jamal and Ivan. It didn't take too long for them to pick out a chain each.

Okay, Ma'am, that's eight thousand, five hundred.

Just run it through my card.

They all laughed as they left the store.

Next stop lingerie, Jamal! I will go to Victoria's Secret.

Linda gave the boys a show.

Do you like it Jamal?

Yeah, darling.

How about you, Ivan?

Looks hot!

Both of you stop it!

What, I can't have anyone else, Jamal? I'm going to take her boyfriend too.

Linda and Ivan laughed.

If you're cool with it, Jamal, said Ivan.

Guess I'm going to have to be.

Ivan and Linda started to make out.

Where do you guys want to go next?

Hey, let's go to Ian's, said Jamal.

We better go check on Delilah.

No way, I have lots more shopping I want to do, said Ivan.

Whatever, Ivan, said Linda, *let's shop some more.*

When they were done they had spent at least fifteen hundred dollars. Jamal bought his kids a whole new wardrobe, and new baby clothes. He hoped it was a girl; Denise and Jamal already had two boys. If he played his cards right with Linda, he wanted two more with Linda.

Hey, darling, it's about time we had a baby.

Really!

Yeah, really, we've got the ring, you've got three bedrooms at your apartment. It's time, darling, let's go shopping for a crib.

Linda had never been happier. She was eighteen, same age her mother was when she had Linda.

I want a nanny; I'm not changing any poopy diapers.

Whatever, said Jamal. Linda thought she had just won the lottery; she wasn't going back to school.

We better go check on her, guys.

Okay, I'm all shopped out; let's forget the clubs, we had enough fun.

No doubt, man, said Ivan. *You got it made, my man; your girlfriend's a catch.*

I know.

Let's go do the crack now, guys.

Whatever you say, darling.

Delilah was still out of it when they got home.

She okay in there, Linda?

Yeah just fine, probably had her limit, I don't need a dead little daddy girl's on my floor, Ivan.

Yeah, she's no use to us dead. When she's eighteen we have already planned for a baby, but she doesn't need to know about us, Linda.

Sounds fine by me, sweetie.

Jamal was furious. *If you guys want to hook up, do it when I'm not around.*

Forget that; I'm doing it while she's passed out, I like it risky.

Ivan and Linda went to Linda's bedroom and made out.

Delilah dreamt of hell; she saw the man with no eyes on fire in hell.

We're waiting for you, Delilah! We just love your new friends; you'll be staying with them for a while. You'll be spending quality time with your friends.

The apparition disappeared. Delilah woke up with a start and looked at Linda's clock. Three-thirty-three; she had awakened at that time for weeks. She went into the living room, where everyone was smoking something.

What's up, guys?

I got a new ring from Jamal, BFF.

I feel like a princess, Delilah.

You always look like a princess, Linda, said Ivan.

What's that supposed to mean? shouted Delilah.

Relax, Delilah, I don't like clingy women.

Delilah was crushed.

Do you want to do some crack, Delilah?

She's too much of a kid, said Ivan.

No I'm not! I'll l have some crack.

Delilah inhaled and coughed. Everyone laughed.

Don't worry, BFF, first time you will cough; try to inhale more.

Delilah took another hit, and inhaled. Her head was still spinning from the drugs she had taken; she liked the feeling of the drugs.

You need to slow down, girl!

I'm fine, Jamal.

Delilah did not want to look like a kid around her new friends.

No more for you, girl; you're high enough, Delilah.

Why, Ivan?

I don't want you to O.D.

Oh you're right, I'll wait.

Inside Delilah wanted more dope.

CHAPTER NINE

NOT A GOOD INFLUENCE

You know you can move in anytime, Delilah.

Really?

You're sixteen, old enough to move away from Mommy and Daddy.

You're right, Linda, I've got my car and ten thousand coming to me. I'll take out more each month, from my lawyer.

Sounds great; this is going to be too cool.

I know, Linda; I am so glad we became friends.

Delilah's phone rang. Who would be calling at this hour?

Hello Di, is it a bad time?

What do you want, Alice?

Why are you so mad at me? I was just sick.

I don't care; you're a fucking freak!

Delilah hung up. Alice was crying on the other end of the phone. What was wrong with Delilah?

I'll see if I can wake up Mom, thought Alice.

Mom, you awake?

I am now, Ally.

Please, let's have some hot chocolate.

Let me get my robe. What's up, Ally?

I phoned Delilah again; we call each other sometimes early in the morning.

Okay, Ally.

She called me a fucking freak, why, Mom?

Ally, you were sick; that's all you need to know.

I know I didn't have a fever! What happened to me?

Like Father Seamus said you were possessed. Please just be happy you're well.

Back at Linda's, Ivan said, *Delilah, I want to talk to you in private.*

Okay, can we use one of the spare bedrooms, Linda?

Pick a room out; you will need one to put your shit in anyways.

Delilah picked the largest one.

What's up, Ivan?

Will you marry me?

Marry you?

Yeah, sweetie, you're the one.

Of course I'll marry you.

We'll buy the ring later; you'll have to buy it.

No problem, we will go first thing in the morning!

Great!

Delilah and Ivan kissed.

Let me go tell Linda and Jamal.

Guess what, guys!

What? said Linda.

We're getting married. Like I'll wait till I'm eighteen, so we have a long engagement.

That's too cool, way to go, Ivan.

Thought you would like that, Linda!

Well it's going to be at least two years, still time to burn some money, thought Linda. *Well, I'll be your bridesmaid, kiddo.*

Of course you will. My dad will have a big wedding for me, I'm spoiled !

Let's ask for a house for the wedding, Delilah!

Sure, no problem, anything you want, Ivan.

Ivan was in heaven; he didn't love Delilah. He was out for the money and would still have his babes on the side. He was sure Kim would come running back, once she knew he was rich. Kim was the love of his life; he dumped her for the paycheck. They still talked every day. She was still in love with Ivan, she told him three times a day.

What time does the mall open, Linda?

Another two hours, kiddo.

Aren't you excited for us, Linda? Like I think it is time for another toke.

You first, Delilah.

I want the Fentanyl.

Whatever you say, kiddo.

Linda tied her off and injected. Delilah passed out.

What a plan, Ivan, you showed me.

Yeah, Linda, she won't be all yours in the meantime.

Have you met her parents?

NO! I don't really want to; I'll wait till she moves in with you. I'm set for the rest of my life!

Great job, said Jamal.

Let's all go get breakfast.

Linda, we still have lots of food from last night.

I want some McDonald's!

I'll go.

No way, Ivan; am I taking the Porsche?

No way, she's my fiancée; half that car's going to be mine!

Whatever, Ivan!

Here's the keys, man.

Thanks, Jamal. I'll bring you McDonald's after I go see Kim. She's going to freak out! I would not want to be you, dude.

Tough shit, she'll just have to accept it. She will get her benefits, she'll accept it; she accepted me dumping her for Delilah. As long as Kim still loves me, that's what's important.

Ivan left for McDonalds.

Kim was nineteen and madly in love with Ivan. She had been going out with him since she was fifteen, and now she was pregnant. She needed to tell Ivan. The buzzer rang.

Hello?

Let me in, babe.

Oh Ivan, it's you!

Yeah, yeah, let me in!

She let him in.

Hi babe, here's some McDonald's, it's Linda's, but you have it.

How's Delilah?

Good, we got engaged.

What!

We got engaged! How am I going to get my hands on her money without marrying her?

That's true, you'll need it. I'm pregnant!

Great!

You're happy?

Yeah, I am I always told you I wanted a child with you! How far along are you?

Three months, will you take me for my ultrasounds?

Sure, you know I don't love Delilah. In ten years you and I will be together forever, babe, set for life.

Well, I guess I'll have to wait.

That's how I've trained you, babe.

When Ivan returned, Delilah asked, *Where did you go, sweetie?*

Just to McDonald's to get breakfast. I took your car, hope that's all right.

No problem, drive it anytime, you're my fiancé.

Thanks, babe. Can I drive it when we're in it from now on?

Sure, anything for you.

He had her where he wanted her, subservient.

Well, let's go pick out a ring.

I'm so excited, Ivan.

Me too, babe, let's go.

Let's go to Max's, Ivan.

Okay, lead the way, sky's the limit, babe. They all headed for Max's.

Good, there was a different salesman than last night.

Can I please look at a three-carat solitaire?

Of course. Regarding solitaires, let me show you what I have.

They looked at rings for an hour. Everyone was bored except Delilah. She finally decided on a four-carat solitaire.

Don't you love it, Ivan?

Yeah, it's great. Ivan couldn't care less.

Well, how much is it?

Twenty-three thousand.

No problem, here's my VISA.

Ivan watched her put in her PIN, same PIN as the MasterCard. *I'll have to remember that.*

Delilah needed it sized, and it was going to be two hours.

Well, time for more shopping, guys; where do you want to go?

Let's go to Janis's; I'll need a new wardrobe to keep up with my rich friend.

Linda was in her glory. She hid the clothes from last night.

Janis's was packed with all the rich women from New York.

Let's try and see if that stupid bitch gives me a dirty look today.

Hi, Tina, I'm going to need to increase my limit on the account to twenty thousand.

No problem, Ms. Shipley.

Go try on anything you want, Linda.

Don't mind if I do.

Linda shopped for an hour and racked up Delilah's card to five thousand. She had everything she needed. After Delilah left Tina called Trip Shipley at the dealership.

Trip Shipley please.

Who's calling?

It's Tina from Janis's Boutique.

Just hold; I'll see if he can take your call.

Trip, it's Tina from Janis's Boutique; she would like you to take her call.

Put her through. Hi, Janis, what can I do for ya?

Thought you would like to know Delilah was just in here; she increased her account to twenty thousand.

What!

She owes over five thousand.

What did she buy?

A whole bunch of clothes for some girl, I know I have seen her before in here.

It's that Linda, said Trip.

Do you know where she went?

No, Trip, I should have asked.

It's not your fault, Tina; I'm heading off to the mall.

Sorry about this, Trip, but I'll need at least two thousand for a payment today.

Of course, I'll head to your store first.

When Delilah comes home I'm taking away her car, thought Trip. He was going to the mall first to make that payment. He didn't want to affect Shirley's account with the store. She bought all her clothes there. *Wait till she gets home,* said Trip to himself. *She's in big shit.*

Tina, thanks for the call, I'll pay in cash.

No problem, Trip.

Trip went to look for Delilah. Delilah was heading for home with Ivan, Jamal, and Linda. Shirley came running to the door.

Oh, thank God, it's you, Delilah.

Mom, this is Jamal, Ivan, and you already met Linda.

Yes, I met Linda.

Hi Mom!

Watch your mouth, punk.

Wow, sorry, lady!

Mom, don't be rude! He's my fiancé.

What!!

Look at my engagement ring.

Delilah showed off her ring. Linda just laughed. She hated Shirley Shipley; she looked down at her.

Well, Mrs. Shipley, we're here to grab some stuff of Delilah's. She's moving in with me.

Oh no, she's not!

Oh yes I am, Mom; get out of my way before I hit you.

Linda and Ivan laughed.

I don't care how much you hate me; at eighteen we will get married, nothing you can do about it!

Who bought you the ring?

I did, Mom, said Ivan.

You don't have that kind of money; you don't even work.

I am in a band.

Jamal and Linda laughed.

Well I'm off, Mom, see ya.

Delilah left. Shirley called Trip

Trip Shipley speaking.

Trip!

What's wrong, Shirley?

Delilah just came home with Linda, Ivan, and some guy named Jamal. She's moved out.

Moved out! Call the police. I'll be home as soon as I can get there.

Shirley called the police.

Sergeant Dan Wilkes speaking.

Dan, it's Shirley Shipley – she knew his wife Karen from church.

Hi, Shirley, what can I do for you?

It's Delilah, Dan; she came home from her friend Linda's and moved out. I need you to trace her cell.

Can't, Shirley, she's sixteen; she can move out if she likes.

Can you just trace her cell? Please, think of her like you would think of your own daughter.

Okay, Shirley, give me the number.

Shirley was relieved. Trip could go there and talk to Delilah.

Okay, here's the address.

Thank you, Dan.

Trip came through the door.

Trip, I have the address.

Good. I'll call David and we will head to Linda's place.

David was Trip's older brother. He used to box.

The phone rang four times.

Hi, Trip, what's up?

I need your help, David.

With what?

Delilah moved out to her friend Linda's. I need to go get her, and there are two guys with her.

I'll be over in ten minutes.

Don't worry, Shirley; David's coming.

Thank God, Trip!

David arrived eight minutes later. Trip met him at the door.

Thanks for coming, David, let's go. I have the address.

Let's take the Porsche, David.

No problem, Trip.

Trip and David headed for Linda's.

I'll do the talking, David.

Whatever you want Trip.

Someone was leaving the apartment when they headed for the *door*.

Ma'am, hold the door.

No problem.

She held the door for Trip and David. The apartment was three-twenty. Trip banged on the door.

Let me in, Linda!

Oh shit, it's my dad, do I look alright? Delilah asked.

You look fine, said Ivan. She really looked like shit, but Ivan said nothing.

Linda answered the door.

What do you want, Mr. Shipley?

Trip was furious.

I want my daughter, you bitch!

Go away, Dad; I moved in with Linda.

Like hell you will!

Get yourself ready, Delilah, we're leaving.

No I'm NOT! I am sixteen, and I can legally move out!

Over my dead body, Delilah; I'll take the Porsche, and cut off your credit cards.

Then I'll never talk to you again, or Mom. Think about that, Dad!

Get lost, old man, she's engaged to me; at eighteen we're getting married and starting our own family.

Dad, look at my ring.

You little shit!

Ivan just laughed at Trip.

I'm going to knock the fuck out of you, shit head.

Touch me and I'll call the police!

He had Trip cornered.

Dad, I will be home for Sunday supper; I'll see you then,

but you're going have to accept Ivan. I will be bringing him Sunday. He's my future husband. I promise I'll wait till eighteen before I get married and have kids, but I'm quitting school.

What? said David.

I'm quitting school, Uncle David.

Delilah, please think clearly, said David.

What do I need school for? I have two trust funds. One from Granma for two hundred thousand, and one from Grandpa for a hundred thousand. I have already set up the trust fund from Granma; I get ten thousand on Friday. Then I'll get an allowance every month.

Ivan just stared at Trip and David.

Leave, old man, she's mine now.

You little fuck, I'll kill you.

Careful, that's a threat. I can call the police for your uttering a death threat, old man.

Dad, just leave, we will see you for Sunday dinner, Ivan and I both.

Trip had nothing to say.

Be there on Sunday at two, no later, Delilah.

Sure, Dad, as long as Ivan can come. See you guys at two.

Thanks, Dad, said Ivan.

I'm going to have my day with you, boy!

Trip and David left.

Your old man is intense, Delilah. He's going to be a great father-in-law, Ivan, said Jamal.

He'll settle down when I am eighteen and can do whatever I want.

Not go to clubs, Delilah.

What about the Kabana, and Hard Core, Ivan?

Yeah, that's true, but they can't serve you alcohol.

Linda is always good about buying it for me.

True, true, babe. I have to leave, can I take the Porsche?

Where are you going, Ivan?

Don't fuckin whine, you stupid bitch!

I'm going to a rave at the Bronx.

Can I come?

You would never get into the Bronx. You would never get by Trevor at the door. I'm not risking anything for you, Delilah.

Don't worry, Delilah; we have plenty of Fentanyl. We'll just get high.

Okay, Linda.

Ivan and Jamal left for the club.

See you later, Linda.

No problem, Jamal.

Ya wait up for me, Delilah.

Okay, Ivan.

Let's get high, BFF. We'll celebrate you moving in.

Sure, Linda, like you said, let's get high!

Linda tied her off, and injected her with some heroin. Delilah was increasing her tolerance, and she didn't pass out. Delilah was having fun.

Holy shit, this is great, Linda!

I thought you would like that, Delilah.

She would have her hooked by the end of the week.

Want to pick up Kim, Ivan?

No, went to see her already; she's pregnant, no fun. I'll connect with Lisa at the club, brother.

Does she have friends?

Yeah, Shelia's hot, had her too.

You dog, brother!

I know, Delilah's cute and all that but when it comes down to it, she's just my meal ticket. I'll stay with her for money. Kim and I can live happily ever after. She's my soul mate; I can't wait to have a baby with her. Going to have to get Delilah back to school, so I have my days free.

You know it, brother!

Ivan and Jamal hit the club. Ivan went to find Lisa and her friends.

Hey, Lisa.

Hey yourself, boyfriend.

Where's Shelia?

Shooting up in the can.

Go get her, bitch; my friend Jamal needs a girl for for tonight.

Shelia came out of the washroom.

Shelia, meet my brother, Jamal.

How is it going, man?

Better now you're here.

Ivan and Jamal were evil and selfishness personified. They cared only for themselves. Lisa was twenty-one and cared only for herself.

Let's head for the bathroom, babe.

Sounds good to me, Ivan.

You care to join them, Shelia?

How old are you, man?

Twenty-three, sweetie; how old are you?

Twenty-five, and you better have a condom.

Right in my back pocket, never leave home without one.

Sounds good then, Jamal.

Everyone headed for the bathroom, to get up to no good.

Okay, I got what I came for, Jamal, how 'bout you?

Always, brother.

Let's head home, Jamal. See I don't need anything from Delilah but her cash; I got plenty going on.

You know it, brother.

It was two in the morning. Time to head home to their babes.

CHAPTER TEN

BACK TO THE GIRLS

Delilah had fallen asleep. Jamal and Ivan walked in at three-thirty.

The stupid bitch is asleep.

Ivan kicked Delilah in the stomach.

Wake up, you stupid bitch!

I'm sorry, Ivan.

Never fall asleep again when you're waiting for me, bitch.

Ivan slapped Delilah across the face. Delilah was shocked beyond belief.

That's what you get you, stupid bitch, when you piss me off.

Let's go to Denny's, guys, Delilah's paying; she's a rich babe.

No problem, Ivan. Sorry, I'll never fall asleep again when I'm waiting for you.

Better not, bitch.

They headed for Denny's.

Booth or table?

Booth, said Jamal.

Can I have a pint of beer, Delilah?

Don't ask her, ask me. I speak for her.

We'll have two pitchers, said Jamal.

Sounds good to me.

I want a Diet Coke and vodka, said Linda.

She's paying, not me; good you asked me, Linda.

You bet, you're the boss.

Can I take your order?

Sure two pitchers of beer, and a Diet Coke with vodka.
We'll order when you bring the drinks.

What will you have sweetie?

Get her a Diet Coke.

You'll have a salad, Delilah; I don't want a fat girlfriend.

Linda and Jamal laughed at Delilah.

You could stand to lose ten pounds, Delilah. Do it by the
end of the month!

Ten pounds in three weeks!

Start tonight!

I don't think I can do that, love.

Don't worry. I'll get you some crystal meth, Delilah. Kills
your appetite.

Thanks, Linda.

The waitress came back with their drinks.

Call Ian, Linda.

Okay, Jamal.

He'll set you up with some meth, Linda; call him now, Linda.

No problem, Ivan.

Linda called Ian.

Ian, I need a thousand C.D's.

No problem, Linda, happy to get you those C.D.'s.

Where do you want to meet?

Outside at Denny's on Groat Road.

See you in fifteen.

Sure, Ian.

Let's go.

Wait, I need a smoke, Delilah.

Sure, Linda. I need to go to a cash machine, Linda.

There's one in the doorway, Delilah. Get Jamal and me a thousand.

Okay, Ivan, I want a thousand too, said Linda.

Holy crap, I don't know what the limit is on my VISA.

Just get it, Delilah!

Yes, Ivan, I'll try.

Try real hard, Delilah, you don't want to piss me off.

Delilah took the money off her credit cards. She needed to use three cards.

Okay, I've got five thousand.

Sounds good to me, Delilah.

Let's go meet Ian; Delilah, you got the cash, right?

Yeah, no problem, Linda.

Linda was like Ivan and Jamal; she loved being evil.

Got the cash, Linda?

She does, Ian; pay the man, girlfriend.

Delilah gave Ian a thousand dollars.

Take the product, retard.

Here's the product, gorgeous.

You hold till we get to my place, Delilah.

Sure, Linda.

Should I put it in my purse, Linda?

Of course, retard, where else?

Sorry, Linda, this is all new to me.

No problem, retard.

Don't call me that!

Whatever, Delilah.

I want to go to the car; I have my pipe in my purse.

Okay, Linda, whatever.

Don't use my expression, retard.

Linda and Delilah went to get high in Delilah's car. Delilah loved crystal meth immediately.

Why did you take so long, bitch?

We went to get high, Ivan.

No problem, Linda, but next time don't take so long.

Delilah went to give Ivan a kiss.

Not in public, bitch!

Sorry, Ivan.

You are a retard, Delilah.

Everybody laughed at Delilah. Delilah wanted to cry, but held it back.

Can I take your order now?

Sure, beautiful.

The waitress blushed. Ivan, Linda, and Jamal ordered a hundred dollars in food.

We'll take some home. Go pay the lady, Delilah.

Sure, Ivan, said Delilah.

Leave her a twenty-dollar tip.

Delilah used her debit card; she had two thousand in her savings and five thousand in her checking account.

Let's go back to my apartment, and do some meth, guys.

Sure, Linda, said Delilah.

We'll do all night, said Ivan and Jamal.

Well least I got Fentanyl to come down.

Who needs to come down? Let's party, guys! said Jamal.

I'm down with it, guys, said Delilah.

You know you really do sound like a retard, Delilah. Everyone laughed at Delilah.

Well, I'm new with the lingo.

Whatever, bitch.

Why do you keep calling me a bitch?

Because I call all my women that, get used to it or go your own way.

Delilah knew he meant it.

Sorry, Ivan, you should use bitch. Linda, you call her retard.

I'll call her bitch.

Sounds good to me, Ivan. They all cracked up except for Delilah.

Delilah loved crystal meth; it made her feel powerful.

This is great, guys.

I know, said Linda, *wait till we do Special K, you can buy it tomorrow.*

No problem, girlfriend.

Delilah was such an easy mark, thought Linda.

Linda, do a show for us, try out that new lingerie.

Whatever, Jamal, let me go get it.

Linda put on the pink one and gave the boys a show.

Delilah looked out the balcony window and saw a dark robed figure.

Look, you guys, out the balcony window! When everybody looked they saw nothing.

What are you talking about, bitch?

I really saw something!

It's the meth, first time, like the Fentanyl, you hallucinated, Delilah.

Oh, sorry, Linda.

That's alright, retard.

Delilah started to cry.

What's the matter, baby? Truth hurts, baby, said Ivan.

You guys stop it now!

Fuck you, Delilah, said Linda; *let's do some more, Ivan.*

Linda knew she had Delilah in the palm of her hand.
Girls can be just as cruel as men, or crueler.

Let's have some left-over lobster, Linda?

Sure, I'll get it out of the fridge, guys.

Well, it's women's work, Jamal, let Linda get it!

Whatever, said Linda.

Warm up some fresh butter, Linda, said Jamal.

Watch it, Jamal, I'm not your wife!

You're his ho; do as he asked, Linda.

Delilah was shocked but didn't say anything. She didn't want to upset Ivan.

You go do it, retard!

Okay, I will, said Delilah.

They all laughed at Delilah. Delilah didn't cry this time; she was too scared of Ivan.

Thanks, retard, said Jamal.

Delilah didn't want to upset anyone. She was becoming afraid of everyone.

Warm up some pizza and Chinese food, retard, said Linda.

Sure, Linda.

That's my BFF, said Linda.

Only Delilah didn't eat; she was the only one doing the meth. Linda wanted to watch her get all fucked up. She got a kick out of Delilah when she was fucked up on drugs. Linda was nowhere near as pretty as Delilah, but she had a killer body. Well the crystal meth would take care of Delilah's beauty. It happens to the greatest lookers. In a couple of months Delilah would look like a hag.

At home Alice was having a terrible nightmare. She dreamed Delilah was in Hell. She was haunted by Delilah's appearance; she looked like a hag. What was happening to Delilah? She was going to see Shirley and Trip in the morning. She just knew they would have the answer.

Morning took forever. She loved her new haircut; she looked good. Now it was just her teeth that needed fixing.

She was not going to school till they were done. Her friend Audrey brought home her homework, so she had something to do with her days and could catch up. Alice was very smart like her dad. She wanted to follow in his footsteps and be a doctor. She wanted to be a pediatrician.

Morning, Ally.

Morning, Mom.

Alice's mom was always up with Alice in the morning now.

Mom, can you drive me to the Shipleys' house this morning?

Did you make the coffee, Alice?

Sure did, Mom.

Wait, I need to have coffee and a bath first.

Sounds good to me, Mom.

Just give me an hour.

No problem, here's your coffee.

Thank you, Alice.

Elizabeth took a long bath. She was still using her drugs, but they got her through the day. She blow dried her hair and thought she needed some make-up this morning. She was usually just a natural beauty like Alice.

Let's go, Alice.

Thanks, Mom.

So what do you need to see the Shipleys about?

Delilah!

That's what I thought.

They pulled up to the Shipleys'. All the lights were on, and Trip's car was still there.

Looks like Trip's still home; that's weird, Alice.

No doubt, Mom.

They rang the doorbell, and Trip came to the door.

Good morning, Alice, Elizabeth.

Sorry we're so early, Trip, said Elizabeth. *Alice would like to see Delilah before school.*

We're sorry, guys; Delilah moved out yesterday.

What? said Elizabeth.

Yeah, she moved in with Linda Banks.

Linda Banks? She is trouble, Mr. Shipley, said Alice.

Don't we know that? said Shirley. *She's coming for dinner on Sunday.*

Please come and talk to her.

No problem, Mr. Shipley.

She's always so kind, Elizabeth.

Trip started to cry.

Don't cry, Mr. Shipley; things will work out.

Did we tell you she's engaged?

What! said Alice.

Yeah, to that Ivan Rider.

Who's Ivan Rider, Mr. Shipley?

I thought you might know him, Alice.

I have no idea. The only Ivan I know is Ivan Dubrowski;

he used to go out with Kim Fields. He is about twenty-three, a big-time bully.

What! said Shirley.

He used some aliases when he hung out at the school. Maybe that's the same guy. What would Delilah want with him? He's a real creep.

I have no idea, Alice, said Trip.

Where is she now?

Living with Linda Banks, like we said, Alice.

Good God! We have to do something!

I already tried. She is sticking by her man, Alice.

He's no man; he's a punk.

Trip and Shirley laughed at that.

Well, it's good to see the old Alice back.

What do you mean the old Alice? I have always been the same Alice!

I mean when you were sick. Thanks, Alice, for trying to help Delilah.

I'm not finished, Mr. Shipley. Give me Linda Banks' address. After I see Father Robert, I am going to see Delilah.

Thank you, Alice; I'm sorry I upset you.

I just wish people would be honest with me.

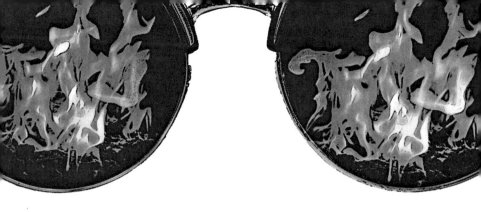

CHAPTER ELEVEN

THE ANSWERS

Father Robert was finishing up with his Mass. He spotted Alice and Elizabeth in the front row. Alice waited until Father Robert was done with communion. She took the Blood and Body of Christ.

She waited patiently for Mass to be over. Father Robert was saying goodbye at the doors.

Father Robert, we need to talk.

Okay, Alice, back in the rectory.

Alice followed him into the rectory. Father Seamus was there, and so was Sister Mary.

Thank you so much, Fathers, Sister Mary. What happened to me?

That boy Brian that came through the board, tis never a boy! You and Delilah invited him to appear.

The demon came through like in The Exorcist *by William Peter Blatty?*

I think I've seen it, said Father Robert.

I have, said Father Seamus, *brilliant movie. Based on a true story, Father Robert.*

Are you trying to tell me I was like Regan MacNeil?

Exactly, Alice, said Father Seamus.

Alice dropped in the chair. Everything went black; then the lights returned.

My God, I did this all to myself.

Yes, Alice, said Father Robert. *It was not you, it was the demon.*

In The Exorcist *the demon's name was Pazuzu. What was the demon in me named?*

Everyone turned to Father Seamus.

Its name was ABIGOR. Do you know how blessed you are child?

How, Father Seamus?

The light of Christ covered you. That's how blessed you are.

What do you mean, Father Seamus, the light of Christ?

The light of Christ came through as a blinding white light, and commanded ABIGOR to depart.

No way, Father Seamus!

It's true, you are meant to be a nun, and help the people in Africa.

Tis true, saw it myself, in a vision.

A nun, hey?

That's correct; my visions always come to pass, said Sister Mary.

This is a lot to take in!

Of course it is, luv, and good won in the end. Some people aren't so lucky, said Sister Mary.

People have died in some cases. The Exorcism of Emily Rose, *true story. Her name in real life was Anneliese Michel.*

No way, Father?

Yes, it's true; she died because the demon would never let her eat.

It's really another true story?

Well it does say in the beginning of the movie, it is based on a true story.

I missed that. Delilah and I were late; we missed the opening credits.

Well no need to talk about Anneliese Michel. She chose her path. Like the movie said, she chose to stay possessed, so we could see the Devil and God really exist.

That's right, the Mother of God came to help her; she chose to stay.

That's correct, Alice.

What happened to me?

You said you watched The Exorcist!

I did!

You missed when Regan was playing with the board?

Captain Howdy came through; there never was a Captain Howdy.

Oh, I'm starting to see this was my fault. I played with the Ouija board with Delilah.

Tis no one's fault. You were ignorant of the board, said Sister Mary.

I should not have! Like Father Seamus said, in The Exorcist, *they do show a board in the beginning of the movie, and Regan talks about Captain Howdy. I never connected the dots.*

Don't beat yourself up over it. Did you get rid of the board?

We tried! Delilah and I threw it away in her garbage at her house; it reappeared in my room.

So you put it away.

How did you know, Father Robert?

I found it in your closet.

Oh I see now, Brian was like Captain Howdy.

Correct, Alice, said Father Seamus, *it was always a demon.*

It was my fault. He told me he wanted to appear and he said he needed an invitation. Delilah and I gave it an invitation.

That's correct, said Father Robert.

How stupid could I be?

Please, Alice, don't go on about it; just tell people what really happened. I have been an Exorcist since I was twenty-four, I am fifty-two and a half. That's twenty-eight years, and I have never had Saint Michael show up in an Exorcism. You truly need to pray and listen to God, Alice.

My friend Delilah, what's happening to her?

She is under oppression, we talked to her, and her dad. They were skeptical, but Mr. Shipley came around. I'm sorry to say Delilah never did; possession is next for Delilah.

Oh my Lord, can you stop it?

We all tried; Delilah was to go to church, three times a week, and confess her sins. She showed up one time for Mass, and never confessed her sins!

She's very stubborn, Father Seamus. She is also very foolish.

Will you please come with me to see her?

Yes, of course, Alice, said Father Seamus.

Of course we will, said Sister Mary and Father Robert.

Ivan Dubrowski is a pretty tough guy. That's Delilah's boyfriend.

I'll call Ken, he's still on a leave of absence from work. He's very strong, but that story is for another time.

Father Seamus called Ken.

Hello, Dr. Darby speaking.

Ken, it's Father Seamus; can you help me out?

Of course, anything for you, Father.

I need some muscle for a job. It's Delilah Shipley.

What's up with Delilah?

She's running with a bad crowd. We need to see her. She's moved out and got engaged to a twenty-three-year-old man named Ivan Dubrowski.

What? Delilah?

Afraid so, she also played with the Ouija board, do you remember?

Yeah, I do remember, Father Seamus.

Remember I told you she was under oppression.

Yes I do!

Well I'm going to try once again to get through to her.

Sure and you need me as back-up.

Yeah, I do.

I will pick you guys up in my Ford Escape, said Ken; *give me an hour, okay?*

Sure, no problem.

He is coming in an hour, enough time for all of us to do the rosary.

Of course, Robert.

Thank you, Father Seamus.

Father Seamus, I have no rosary.

Plenty in the rectory, Alice.

Thanks, Father Robert. I'm embarrassed I don't remember anything after Holy Mary Mother of God.

I'll help ya, luv, said Sister Mary.

Thank you, Sister Mary; maybe one day I'll be wearing a habit like you.

I'm sure you will, Alice.

This will be a homework assignment, Alice.

Yes, Father Seamus.

Ken entered the rectory.

Your muscle's here, Father Seamus.

Thank you so much, Ken, for coming.

Anything for you, Father Seamus.

I'm going to get a fat head, Ken.

You got the address, Father Seamus?

Alice has it, Ken.

Okay let's roll. Give me the address, Alice.

Alice gave Ken the address.

Alice was thinking about how happy Ken used to make her mother. In her childish way she had given him a hard time. She wished she could take it back, so she would pray for it. Ken never held it against her; he took a leave of absence from work to help her parents out with her. Granma said he was the best out of all them. He only lost it once with the demon. Otherwise he was the calmest of all of them all. Typical, he was coming out to Linda's.

Everybody cheer up a bit; we had enough sour faces at the Exorcism.

Sorry, Ken, you're right, I should be counting my blessings, said Father Seamus. *I am just a wee bit scared.*

Don't be; I'm a boxer, street fighting expert, and have my black belt. I know how to disarm any weapon from anybody. I have to with my forensic patients. Talk about evil. I have really been thinking about some of my patients. Some of them I'm sure are possessed.

Well that's a leap of faith, Ken, good for you seeing it in a new light.

But it's still terrifying.

That never changes, Ken, said Sister Mary. *Let's go, guys!*

CHAPTER TWELVE

IVAN THE TERRIBLE

L inda was in a foul mood today. She couldn't locate any Fentanyl or heroin. Nobody was holding and Ivan kept her busy in the bedroom all night. Ivan was still sleeping, so she and Delilah were walking on pins and needles.

Delilah could hear them all night. Delilah wondered what had changed between her and Ivan; when he was courting her he was such a gentleman. Now he was very mean to her.

She said to herself that she had to be a better girlfriend to him. She understood that he had needs. He wanted to wait till they were married at eighteen before any physical relationship took place.

She was the maddest at Linda; she was walking around in her Victoria's Secret lingerie last night, and she drove Ivan nuts. He was a hot-blooded male, and she knew it. When Jamal left, she was all over Ivan. They both were laughing.

Linda, get in here right now.

Whatever, hold on, Ivan, I wanted some more meth.

Linda took a drag from her pipe, giggled in Delilah's direction and went to see Ivan.

Hi Ivan.

Hey, babe, come here and warm me up. I'm cold.

No problem, I can help you with that.

What time was Delilah up this morning? Was she up at six like I told her?

No, she slept till nine.

Delilah had never even gone to bed – Linda wanted Ivan to beat her. She enjoyed it.

Hold on, babe.

She went out with Ivan. Delilah heard them coming and cringed.

Get up, you stupid lazy bitch.

What's wrong, Ivan?

Ivan kicked her hard in the shin. Delilah started to cry.

Look at the baby crying, Linda.

Too funny, sweetie.

Shut up, you stupid cunt!

Delilah stopped crying instantly. Ivan and Linda headed back into the room; when Linda reached the door she turned around and laughed.

Delilah was starting to hate Linda with a passion. It turned her on, turned both Ivan and Linda on, to torture Delilah. They always had great sex after Ivan beat Delilah. Linda could not stand how cute Delilah was, or her innocence.

Delilah thought about leaving and returning home. Even if she wanted to, she couldn't; she was scared what Ivan and Linda would do to her or her parents. She also missed Alice. Alice was always so kind to Delilah, except when she was sick. She was just sick; Delilah was too scared to look at the other possibilities.

Ivan and Linda came out of the room. They went to the living room and turned on the TV. That was another thing Delilah was not allowed to do anymore – to watch TV.

Order me a pizza and a case of beer, Delilah.

Sure Ivan; Linda, do you want anything?

Yeah, two orders of spaghetti, one for now and one for later, with extra cheese.

Okay, guys, do you want it from Rocky's?

"Do you want it from Rocky's?" No, ya bitch. The Pasta Garden, you can order it; then I'll pick it up. Ya retard, also I want six bottles of their best champagne, laughed Linda.

She knew it was top of the line champagne at one hundred twenty-five dollars a bottle. Linda loved Pasta Garden, but the cost of the food was out of her price range. Not anymore, she could have anything she wanted with Delilah's dad's money.

I want that ten grand you're getting on Friday, Delilah.

What?

You heard me, the ten grand you get on Friday, bitch.

Don't worry, Linda; I'll give you and Jamal two thousand.

Alright, sweetie.

The doorbell rang.

Go answer it, retard.

Delilah answered it.

Where's Linda? asked the man at the door.

Linda, this gentleman wants to speak to you.

What do you want, Peter?

Jamal has not paid this month's rent or last month's rent.

That stupid asshole.

Linda didn't even ask Delilah. She went to Delilah's purse and grabbed her wallet. Delilah watched in shock.

I'll pay for a year in advance, and take the money for the two months' rent in arrears. Also I'll give you two hundred for your trouble.

Sounds fair, Linda, sorry about the inconvenience.

Peter, this is my new roommate, Delilah. She will be taking care of the power bill too.

Nice to meet you, Delilah.

Nice to meet you, Peter.

Don't talk to her; she's a retard.

Peter felt sorry for Delilah. She looked like she was going to cry.

Like I said, Delilah, nice to meet you.

You too, Peter.

Linda went up to Delilah and slapped her across the face. Delilah started to cry; she just wanted to go home.

Why did you hit me, Linda?

'Cause Jamal pissed me off.

I am leaving, you guys; I'll go to the office and collect my card on the way out.

You're not going anywhere, bitch; grab her, Linda.

Linda grabbed her by the hair – Linda was very strong. They dragged Delilah down the hallway by her hair and threw her into bathroom.

Get a kitchen chair.

They locked her in the bathroom.

Let me out of here, screamed Delilah.

When you learn to behave, retard.

There is no way we are going to let you leave, bitch!

Linda grabbed the door and flung it open.

Give me the ring!

Delilah took off the ring off her finger.

Don't think we're still engaged; I don't want to marry you bitch!

That's fine, Ivan; just let me leave, guys. I won't tell anybody.

You can't leave! We own you, Linda spit at Delilah.

Go grab a knife, Linda.

Linda came back with a very large knife.

I need to change the lock on the spare bedroom. We will lock it on the outside; watch her close, Linda.

I will, sweetie. Move and I'll cut your throat.

Delilah was so scared she wet her pants.

Gross retard, she pissed her pants, Ivan.

What a pig, Linda.

No doubt, hurry with the door, Ivan.

It's done.

They threw Delilah into the room and locked the door.

Don't make a sound, or we will cut your throat, said Linda.

Delilah was terrified she was going to die. She cried silently. She was so stupid, thinking they would just let her go home. She *was* a retard.

Let's go shopping, Ivan.

Good idea.

She's not going anywhere soon.

See you in about five hours, retard.

Delilah checked the window, it was a window that only cranked open; there was no way to escape. She thought about screaming out the window for for help, but she was scared. The window was facing the parking lot; what if they were waiting in the car to see if she would cry for help, and then come in and beat her. It was only two more days until she and Ivan were going to her parents', she would make her move then, and leave Ivan. The buzzer went off in the apartment, but she had no way to get to it.

Peter was downstairs in the entrance way, watering some plants.

Excuse me, sir, I was wondering if you could let us in the building?

Why?

We came to visit a friend, Linda Banks; she lives in apartment three-twenty.

Just saw Linda leaving; she's out. She told me on the way out she had some people harassing her, and not to let anyone into the building. She said tenants are just letting anyone through the doors. That's not our policy in the building.

Well, we believe she has another girl living with her; we need to see her – it's urgent.

She has a guest staying with her, some girl, can't remember the name.

Her name is Delilah; that's who we really need to see.

Well, she's not on the lease, can't let you in to see anyone.

We think she needs our help.

She's in there, just saw her up there; if she needs help she'll let you in.

We tried calling but she's not answering.

Then she doesn't need your help.

As you can see we are priests; why would Father Robert and myself be harassing her?

Makes no difference to me; she might even be needing your help. Go get the police; that's the only persons I can be letting in. I am very sorry, Fathers.

Can you then please ring the buzzer, or better yet go knock on the door? Tell her Father Robert is here to see her.

Guess no harm in that, just give me a second.

Peter went to the apartment and knocked on the door. *Delilah, you in there? I need to talk to you.*

Delilah heard Peter at the door and was just about to yell out to him to let her out. *What if it's a set-up? Peter seemed pretty cozy with Linda after she gave him the two hundred dollars. What if he is knocking on the door, to set up a trap. Better not to take the chance. Linda and Ivan would just laugh at her and give her a beating, or possibly slit her throat. Better to stay quiet.*

Well I tried; she is not answering the door. She would have let me in. I need twenty-four hours, without the tenant's permission, to go inside the suite. Been good tenants, except for last couple of months, got behind on the rent.

Peter was apologetic about the situation, and cleared it right up. *Get the cops if it's that important to you.*

Well thanks anyway, said Father Robert.

They left the building. If she needed, or wanted to see them, she would have answered the door. They couldn't go to the cops, she was entitled to refuse to see them because she was of legal age to move out.

Well guys, we tried, I just wish we could have helped.

Father Robert, at least you tried. She legally can move. If we continue to bother her we're the ones the police are going to be steamed at. Worse yet we could be charged with harassment. That would we be very bad for all of our careers.

This is true, I am not even a citizen. I would never be allowed back in the States.

We better just accept the decision. Trip told me she is coming on Sunday. She may even come back on her own, it has to be her decision.

They drove away.

Linda and Ivan pulled up in the parking lot. Peter was in the parking lot ready to drive away. He stopped when he saw the car.

Hey guys, some people were at the door of the building, wanted to see Delilah.

Who were they? asked Linda.

Some blond-haired guy, looks like that vampire on True Blood, *that Eric guy. He had two priests and a red haired girl with them.*

They're some of the people harassing Delilah. That's why she staying with us, we're helping her.

Oh, well, she is going to have to sign the lease.

No problem, come back when you have a new lease made up. Delilah is probably really happy you didn't let them in.

Do you still have that card we gave you?

Sure do, you need it back?

Yeah, but only after you've put another five hundred dollars on it. I'm sure Delilah will have no problem with that.

Sounds good, I'll see you in a half an hour, with the new lease.

Sounds great, Peter.

We need to get through Delilah's head we're very serious about her seeing these people.

Delilah heard them coming through the door; they walked up to the bedroom door.

Hello bitch, hello retard, had some friends drop by, even brought a couple of priests, clever. We need for you to understand if one more person comes to see you, we are going to take some pretty serious steps with your family, and friends. If we would cut your throat what makes you think we won't cut someone else's throat? Come here, you retarded bitch, time for another beating, looks like we're going to have to beat some sense into you. Gives us great joy to punish you.

Linda went to get the knife and scissors. She cut Delilah's hair, and Ivan gave her a beating.

Okay bitch, you're going to call your dad, and tell him you have decided not to come see him due to his interfering in your life.

Delilah was truly afraid for her friends and family, so she called her dad.

Trip, I have a call from your daughter; she said it was important.

Trip's heart filled with joy.

Hello honey, thanks for calling.

Dad, Father Robert and that other priest came looking for me. They brought Alice and I think Ken.

Don't accuse a person if you don't know who they are.

Well, the landlord said he looked like Eric off True Blood. *Ken's the only person that I know who looks like Eric. Leave me and my friends alone before we charge you with harassment. I also won't be coming on Sunday.*

Delilah hung up the phone. Trip shut the door to his office and cried – then he stopped crying. Something about the conversation didn't make sense, Delilah sounded unhappy; why did it sound like she was reading from a script. When Delilah was mad she always screamed – there was no screaming. It made him stop and think, was there someone who was telling her to make the call? Trip was always going to call, maybe she would understand when she had her own children.

Good, it sounded believable, retard; ya stupid bitch, you're getting better at understanding we mean business.

Delilah did understand that they meant what they said; they really wanted to hurt someone.

Please stop threating my family; it's obvious you mean what you say. If you're going to hurt someone, hurt me.

Oh we will, we will hurt you AND your family. Like we keep telling you, we enjoy suffering. How do you like your knew haircut?

Let's take her, Ivan.

Ivan grabbed her arm and dragged her down the hallway.

Pretty, isn't it, retard; are you going to cry, bitch?

That's one thing she was never going to do again was cry – they liked it too much.

Your cell phone is really starting to piss us off.

Linda took her cell phone and smashed against the wall.

She was being held against her will, trapped by three maniacs. Why were they doing this to her? Was this the first time they did this, or had they done this before? They were just standing there giving her a malevolent look.

Why are you doing this to me?

Because we can! That's why, said Ivan.

You were so stupid to think I could like a stuck-up bitch like you, said Linda.

Where's that ring, Linda?

Why?

I want to give to it to Kim.

I want it!

You've got a ring, don't be selfish.

Whatever, it's in my jewelry box, I'll get it.

I'm going to go give it to Kim; watch the stupid bitch.

Linda enjoyed being in the position of power.

Come on, retard, time to clean the apartment. Or do you even know how to clean? You spoiled bitch, I bet you have a cleaning lady, right, bitch!

Delilah said nothing. Linda slapped her across the face.

Answer me, retard, do you have a cleaning lady?

Yes, we have a maid.

Must be nice to be rich. It looks like that's going to change for me, retard. Take off all your jewelry, give it to me.

Delilah took off her one-carat diamond earrings her mother gave her for her sixteenth birthday. She also gave her a gold watch, a ten thousand dollar emerald ring, and a five thousand dollar ruby necklace.

They will look nice on me, much better than they look on you, skank.

Linda put on all the jewelry.

This is too fun! How do they look on me, retard?

They look nice, Linda.

I know, said Linda. Linda slapped Delilah across the face.

Phone that bitch Alice, tell her you never want to see her again. Do it now!

You broke my phone.

I'll get you a phone, retard.

Delilah phoned Alice.

Hello, Alice, it's me, Delilah.

Delilah I'm so glad you called.

Leave me alone, and don't come around my new apartment. You're not welcome.

What's wrong with you, Delilah?

Nothing, I just don't want to be your friend.

Give me the phone, retard. Alice, you crazy freak, don't ever show your ugly face around my apartment again. I'm Delilah's best friend now, freak.

Linda hung up the phone. Alice cried. Alice went over to the Shipley house.

Hi, Mrs. Shipley.

Hello, Alice, come in.

I talked to Delilah this morning.

What did she say?

She told me she no longer wanted to be my friend. That her and Linda wanted me to leave her alone.

Delilah said that?

Yes she did.

I don't know what's wrong with Delilah. That Linda has been a terrible influence. She was supposed to come over on Sunday; she called and cancelled. I'm sorry, Alice, how are you feeling?

All in all not bad.

We kept you in our prayers, especially Delilah.

Thank you, Mrs. Shipley. I think that Ouija board brought evil into both Delilah's and my life.

I think you're right, Alice.

Ivan went over to Kim's place to give her the engagement ring. Ivan rang Kim's buzzer.

Hey babe, let me in.

Okay babe.

Kim buzzed him up.

What's up?

Nothing I just feel sick all the time.

Well, I've got something that's going to make you feel better.
Ivan gave Kim the ring. *Told you I was going to marry you.*

Oh my God, look at the size of it. Where did you get the money for it?

My rich bitch. Said I was getting it for her, well she got it for herself. I was never going marry that stupid bitch. Let's go to the bedroom.

No Ivan, I'm sick.

Well I guess I'll need to find a new bitch to give it to me!

Don't be like that, Ivan.

Listen, if you're going to do this throughout your pregnancy, I need to find a replacement for you for a while.

You're an asshole.

You're a stupid bitch. I get nothing for the ring! Fuck you; I'm leaving.

Ivan stormed out. Kim sat down and cried.

CHAPTER THIRTEEN

THE RETURN

Everyone was tired from the day. Alice was trying to recoup her energy. She had lost a lot of weight, and was tired most of the time. She couldn't help but feel very sorry for Delilah. What had happened to her? Linda Banks was a very rough character. Ivan was even tougher. Why did she have to play with that board? She never would have thought this was all going to happen.

Alice wanted a warm bath and to go to bed. Alice ran a bath and put her good bubble bath and bath salts into the tub. She had lost so much weight she was cold all the time. She stepped into the tub; she always enjoyed her baths. She was relaxing in the tub when she heard a moan. She tried to pinpoint where the noise was coming from. She heard it again; it was coming from the vent in the bathroom. She jumped out of the tub. She felt hands around her waist, wrist, stomach, and her throat. She couldn't breathe. Everything started to go black, then she felt pressure at the top of her head. She tried to scream, but couldn't. Everything went black.

Alice? Alice?

The bathroom door blew open. Elizabeth watched in horror as Alice floated on top of the water in the tub.

She is ours, don't touch her, you swine! Elizabeth screamed.

LEGION STILL HAS A DEBT TO BE REPAID.

Alice bent backwards and floated on top of the water.

Ryan! Ryan! Come help me, bring the Holy Water.

Ryan grabbed the Holy Water and ran up the stairs. He looked upon Alice in awe.

I can't move, Ryan!

SHE IS STILL GOING TO THE PIT!

Alice turned her head to the side, *HELLO, MOMMY, DADDY.*

What's going on, Ryan?

I don't know, I thought this was finished.

Alice dropped into the water. Her head went under the water, and Ryan sprinkled Holy Water on top of the tub water.

NICE TO SEE YOU, SCUM. THIS HAS BECOME QUITE THE WAR, PLANKTON.

Why are you still here? You were banished, ABIGOR! Who are you?

THAT IS FORBIDDEN. I AM THE COMMANDER OF OTHER LEGIONS; I COMMAND DIFFERENT LEGIONS THAN ABIGOR HAS CONTROL OVER. I'M PICKING UP. WHEN ABIGOR WAS BANISHED,

I WAS TOLD BY MY FATHER TO PICK UP WHERE HE LEFT OFF.

Ryan went to grab Alice, and he sprinkled her with Holy Water. Alice fell into Ryan's arms; they dressed Alice and placed her in bed.

Call Father Robert, Elizabeth.

Elizabeth grabbed the phone and dialed Father Robert's number. The phone rang three times.

Hello, Father Robert speaking.

Father Robert, it's not over!

What?

Please come quickly.

Father Robert did not know what to say or what to do. He woke up Father Seamus.

Father Seamus, Father Seamus, wake up; it's not over.

What are you talking about, man?

Elizabeth O'Doyle called and said it's not over.

Father Seamus sat straight up in bed.

Ya can't be serious, man.

I am, we're to come right now!

I will have to call Sister Mary, but I will wait till tomorrow. Let's get back to the house.

They called Father Patrick, and he picked them up in twenty minutes.

This is another twist I just don't understand, I mean the command came from Saint Michael himself, Father Robert.

Father, you're the expert, but is the Devil not still at war with God?

True, Father Robert. I'm starting to believe Alice is someone very special. She is touched by God. I'm glad I waited to contact the Archdiocese.

Yes, thank God we waited, said Father Robert.

They arrived in half an hour. Ryan answered the door.

Hello, Fathers, she is upstairs.

Father Seamus and Robert went to Alice's bedroom. Alice was sitting in her rocking chair.

OUR WAR WITH GOD IS NOT OVER. WE LOST THE BATTLE, BUT NOT THE WAR.

Who are you, demon?

A FRIEND OF MINE TOLD ME ABOUT HER.

You will be banished too, said Father Robert.

WE WILL SEE YOU, LITTLE MAGGOT.

Father Seamus, Father Robert, what is happening to our child? asked Elizabeth.

This is still a mystery, said Father Seamus. *Please, Ryan, get some rope.*

Good God not again, said Elizabeth.

This time there was no resistance from Alice.

I'm so sorry, Ryan, but I need to call Ken.

That's alright, Lizzy; he has been a part of this from the beginning.

Elizabeth was very worried about her codependence on Ken. She thought of Ken before her mother. Elizabeth went to make the call. Ken answered after two rings.

Dr. Darby speaking.

Ken, it's Elizabeth; please come over right now.

I'll come; don't cry, Elizabeth.

Ken was there in fifteen minutes. Elizabeth answered the door.

Thank you, Ken; it's not over.

What?

The Fathers are up with her now.

Ken went upstairs.

Fathers, what's up?

Ken saw Alice and knew.

What went wrong, Fathers?

We don't know, Ken, said Father Seamus.

NICE TO SEE YOU DOCTOR. YOU REALLY WANT YOUR CAKE AND EAT IT TOO. WE WANT THE SAME THING. LUST IS EVIL. YOU WANT THE MOTHER AND WE WANT HER DAUGHTER.

Ken was stunned.

Don't listen to it, Ken, it's a trickster, said Father Robert.

NEVER UNDERESTIMATE MY POWER, FATHER ROBERT. WE ARE OLDER THAN CHRIST.

You're beneath Christ, demon, said Father Seamus.

YOU THINK BECAUSE YOU'RE A PRIEST YOU KNOW ANYTHING ABOUT THE WAR. OUR WAR IS NOT OVER THE CHILD BUT WITH GOD.

We must take a break to make a up a plan of action, Father Robert, then we must continue the Rite.

Yes, Father Seamus.

Everyone went to the kitchen.

I hate to have to do this, Ryan, but we need to phone my mother. She would never forgive us if we didn't.

Call her, Elizabeth.

Mom, Alice is sick again.

What do you mean, bubble?

Alice is still possessed.

What?

Just come, Mom.

Give me an hour, bubble.

Eileen threw some clothes on and called a cab.

Oh Mom, we were so happy today.

I know, Elizabeth; we will be happy again. Can I see my granddaughter?

Mom, wait, okay?

Okay, are the Fathers here?

Yes and so is Ken.

You love that man, bubble.

Elizabeth turned her head.

Don't cry, bubble, but you have to think long term after this tragedy.

Eileen walked into the kitchen.

Why is this happening, Father Robert?

We don't know, Eileen.

Please, everyone, trust in our Lord; we don't know why this is happening, said Father Seamus.

I have always trusted in our Lord, Father Seamus.

I'm sorry, I didn't mean anything personal, Eileen.

We are all at a loss, said Ken.

Ken, you will never know how grateful this family is.

Thank you, Eileen; I will stay until it's finished.

We must continue on; let's go upstairs, Father Robert.

Yes, Father Seamus.

How should we begin, Father Seamus?

It is an Exorcism; we start again.

FATHER, YOU RETURNED, WHERE'S THE BITCH? WE WANT THE BITCH.

You do not give me commands, demon.

YOU ARE A FOOL, SEAMUS; YOU UNDERESTIMATE ME.

You are an unholy creature, you will fail.

I WILL WAIT FOR THE BITCH.

I will call, Father Robert.

Yes, Father Seamus.

Father Seamus went downstairs to call Mary.

Sister Veronica, let me please speak with Sister Mary.

She is sleeping, Father Seamus.

This is an emergency, Sister Veronica.

Yes, Father Seamus.

What's up, Seamus? said Mary.

It is not finished; get to the O'Doyles!

Yes, Seamus, I will be there in an hour.

Sister Mary was there within the hour.

What's happening, Seamus?

I do not know, Mary; we just must start over again. Like we both know, each Exorcism is different.

I have never heard of it, Seamus, but we know the demonic are very clever.

We at least got to eat something before this happened.

I don't like going without the fast, but it is necessary; come upstairs.

Eileen was shaking beyond control. She was sixty-five, and her age was starting to show.

Eileen, I do not like your shaking, said Ken. *You will need to go on Xanax.*

I don't rely on pills, Ken.

Mother, listen to Ken; he sees this all the time.

Okay, for you to relax, I will, bubble.

Thank you, Mother.

I will phone it into Walmart, and I will pick them up for you, said Ken.

That's much appreciated, Ken

I need to call Brenda at the hospital; she can phone in my prescription.

Ken called Brenda, and phoned in the prescription.

CHAPTER FOURTEEN

FREEDOM

When Ivan came back, he was in a foul mood.

Linda, get in here.

What's your problem, Ivan?

Get rid of Jamal.

Why, Ivan? I love him.

It's me or Jamal!

Okay, okay, babe, calm down.

I want you all to myself, I hate sharing.

You're not ever going to truly leave Kim.

Yes I am. After we're done here – with plenty of money – we hit the road.

Sounds good to me.

Where's the bitch?

Leave the kid alone, Ivan. Listen, if we keep this up we are going to get into trouble. Let's grab some money, then leave. She has plenty of credit cards, and that money should be coming through on her inheritance.

I forgot about that.

They let Delilah out of the room.

Come out, Delilah, said Linda. *You'll need to sell us the Porsche, Delilah.*

That's no problem.

I'll make up the bill of sale, said Ivan.

Good girl, no hard feelings, friend.

When's your ten grand coming through?

Should be in my account.

Well, let's go to the bank and see; I'll drive the Porsche.

Delilah and Linda went to the bank.

Hello, Ms. Shipley.

Hi, Rhonda, I need to withdraw money from my account.

Okay, fill out the withdrawal slip.

Please check my account to see how much is there.

Rhonda checked the account, and wrote down the balance on a piece of paper. Delilah looked at the balance and filled out the withdrawal slip for eleven thousand six hundred and fifty-two dollars.

Please, Rhonda, bring me the cash.

That's a lot of cash, Ms. Shipley.

Give me large bills please, Rhonda.

Okay.

Rhonda, just get the cash.

Rhonda went and got the cash.

Great job, kiddo.

Thank you, Linda.

Ivan and I are leaving with this cash and whatever you can get off your credit cards.

That's great, Linda.

He never stopped loving me, I think. I mean Ivan, Delilah.

I know, Linda.

Delilah would say anything to go home.

I love this car, Delilah.

Yeah, it's great.

I wish it was brand new but this will do. You know it was nothing personal, Delilah, you just made a stupid mistake. I always wanted the money. Why do you think I would hang out with a retarded sixteen-year-old?

I guess I'm retarded, like you say, Linda.

You got that right, well you have that freak of a friend Alice to hang out with. I have twenty thousand dollars, a Porsche, and Ivan.

That's great, Linda.

Delilah and Linda went back to the apartment.

I'm home, babe, got the cash.

Linda and Ivan made out in the living room. Delilah thought she was going to be sick.

Pack, Linda.

I know, babe, I will; we have twenty thousand in cash.

Well, we need to count it for an exact amount.

Twenty thousand!

That's right, babe. Alright, Linda! What are we going to do to keep the bitch from talking?

I won't talk; please just let me go.

Have you made up the Bill of Sale, Ivan?

Yeah, sign it, Delilah.

Okay, Ivan.

Here's your dollar, bitch.

Can I leave now?

When we leave.

Linda got packed.

Give us an hour, then you can leave, not a minute before.

Okay, Ivan.

See ya, retard.

Linda and Ivan left. Delilah waited a long time, what seemed like hours. Delilah went to Peter's office.

Peter, can I use your phone?

Sure, you alright?

Yes, Peter, please don't leave me!

What's wrong, Delilah?

Nothing, I just need a ride.

Where's your car?

I sold it to Linda.

Peter handed Delilah the phone. Delilah called her mom.

Mom!

Oh Delilah, I have been calling your cell, why didn't you answer?

It needed to be charged. Please come and pick me up at the office at Linda's apartment. The address is One Thirteenth and Broadway.

Where's your car?

Mom, please come now.

Okay, Delilah.

I'll just wait here till my mom comes, Peter.

No problem, Delilah.

Delilah saw her mom's car outside.

Thank you, Peter.

No problem, Delilah.

Peter did not ask why she had a black eye.

Oh Mother, thank God you're here!

What happened to your eye, Delilah?

Ivan hit me; just leave this place.

Delilah?

Please, let's just go! Can you call Dad and ask him to come home?

Already have done that, he will be home when we get home.

Shirley and Delilah pulled up in their driveway.

I just want my daddy, Mom.

You're home; everything's all right, Delilah.

Delilah ran into the house.

Daddy! Daddy!

I'm right here, honey. What happened to your eye?

Ivan hit me!

I'll kill him!

What happened, Delilah?

It was awful, Daddy, they held me captive.

I'm phoning the police.

Detective Wilkes speaking.

Dan, come to the house; Delilah has been found, but she was held captive.

Right over, Trip.

Detective Wilkes showed up.

What happened, Delilah?

I was held captive.

Where?

At Linda Banks' apartment.

Who held you captive?

Linda Banks and Ivan Dubrowski.

Ivan Dubrowski?

Yes.

I think I have an outstanding warrant on him. Used to deal drugs.

I had no idea, Detective Wilkes.

He's trouble, how did you get messed up with him?

I was his girlfriend?

Delilah, you have more class than that.

Guess I didn't.

Sorry, Delilah. I don't want to make this worse. Do you want to press charges?

Of course we do, Dan, said Trip.

He has left town with Linda.

We will find them.

They're in my Porsche, Detective Wilkes.

Detective Wilkes left.

Please tell us what happened.

Mom, it was very scary, all he wanted was my money. They robbed me blind is all they did.

They held you captive, Delilah.

I know.

Alice, Father Robert, Father Seamus, and Ken tried to help you.

I know, I was unable to call out to Peter.

Why?

I thought it was a trap.

They will pay for crossing Trip Shipley.

They took a lot of cash like I told Detective Wilkes.

I don't care about the money, we have plenty of money, but only one Delilah.

I want to take a shower, Mom.

Of course, go ahead.

Delilah had an hour-long shower.

She got into her pink flannel PJs. Delilah wanted revenge, but kept it to herself. She went back downstairs, feeling human again.

Daddy, can we order pizza? I'm starved, I haven't eaten in who knows how long.

What cruelty, said Shirley.

How's Alice?

Fine I think, we have not heard from the O'Doyles in days.

Delilah called Alice.

Hello, Dr. O'Doyle here.

Dr. O'Doyle, it's Delilah; I can explain everything.

What happened, Delilah?

I was held captive by Linda Banks and Ivan Dubrowski.

What?

My dad can explain the rest of the story. I need to speak to Alice!

She is sick, if you can really call it sick again.

What? Why?

We don't know.

It was that board!

We know, Delilah. I'm glad you are alright.

Thank you, Dr. O'Doyle.

I really must go now, Delilah; I need to help my own daughter.

Well guys, Delilah is home and safe.

Thank God, said Ken. *What happened, Ryan?*

I only know she was held captive by Ivan Dubrowski and Linda Banks.

I knew there was something wrong, said Ken.

Well, one girl is safe.

Delilah was held captive, and so is Alice

CHAPTER FIFTEEN

An Unwanted Visitor

Why were you sent, demon?

WE ARE NOT FINISHED WITH THE GIRL.

You are an evil, vile abomination.

WE ARE THE SERPENT IN THE TREE – TIME-LESS AND HATEFUL OF THE WHOLE HUMAN RACE. YOU WILL SOON BE THROWN INTO THE LAKE OF FIRE. YOU ARE FOOLS TO THINK GOD CARES FOR THE HUMAN RACE. LOOK WHAT HUMANS DO TO EACH OTHER DAILY. GOD HAS GIVEN UP ON YOU.

You are a liar, demon.

One of the restraints broke loose, and Father Seamus was scratched across his face.

Sister Mary, go downstairs and get Ryan and Ken.

Ryan, Ken, Father Seamus needs your help.

Ryan and Ken ran up the stairs. They saw that Alice had got out of one of the restraints. They held down her hands and restrained her again.

Thank you, gentlemen; we will have to begin the Rite again.
Ryan and Ken left.

Who are you, cruel demon?

I AM THE DEMON WHO WILL TAKE THIS CHILD'S SOUL TO HELL! ABIGOR TOLD ME ABOUT CLARE; MY BROTHERS WILL HAVE A GRAND TIME WITH HER. WE KNOW A LITTLE BIT ABOUT CLARE'S FUTURE. FOLLOWING IN DADDY'S FOOTSTEPS, ANOTHER TROUBLESOME NUN.

This came as a shock to both Father Seamus and Sister Mary. He was scared for her now.

Shut up, demon, give me your name.

NEVER! I'M MUCH STRONGER THAN ABIGOR.

You are subject to God's will, he will not let you take her to hell.

HE WILL HAVE NO CHOICE.

You and Lucifer will be the ones who will have no choice.

WE WILL WIN THE WAR THIS TIME; WE HAVE GREAT POWER, MORE THAN YOU REALIZE, FATHER.

I think you underestimate Christ's power over you and your Legions.

MY FATHER WOULD HAVE GIVEN CHRIST EVERYTHING, BUT THE FOOL CHOSE TO BE NAILED TO A CROSS.

He gave his life so the whole human race would have everlasting life.

WELL HELL IS FULL WITH HIS PEOPLE AND THEY DO NOT WISH FOR EVERLASTING LIFE.

They also did not follow God's law; the human race is subject to his laws – you already know this. I will prove my point. Holy Water, Father Robert.

As soon as the demon felt the Holy Water, it shrieked.

You will be punished greatly for the terror you have caused. You are a robber of life and souls and you will always be subject to his powers. What is your name, foul creature?

FUCK YOU, FATHER!

One of Alice's books was hurled at Father Robert, hitting him in the back of his head.

Are you alright, Father?

Yes, Sister.

Alice's ceiling light fell on Sister Mary.

Help her, Father Seamus!

Get Ryan, Robert!

Father Robert ran as fast as he could down the stairs.

Ryan, please come help Sister Mary; the ceiling light fell down on her. Please tell me that's she's alright, Ryan.

Ryan took her pulse.

Her pulse is strong, but I am going to have to take her to St. Michael's.

Okay, Ryan, thank you.

No problem.

Ken, help me take Sister Mary to my car.

Of course, Ryan. What happened?

The ceiling light in Alice's room fell on Sister Mary. She has a big gash on her head. Let's get her in the car, Ken.

Ken and Ryan got Sister Mary down the stairs to Ryan's car. Ryan drove her to St. Michael's quickly.

Father Robert and Father Seamus continued the Rite. Eileen took another Xanax; this time it made her very tired.

I am going to lie down in the downstairs spare room.

Alright, Mom, you get as much sleep as possible or you're going to get sick.

Ken, go get some sleep.

No, I will not leave you alone, Elizabeth.

Eileen looked at Ken and saw the love he felt for her daughter.

I am going to lie down now, you two.

Please, Mother, get plenty of rest, you're not young like us anymore.

I am going to pull out the sofa bed in the living room, Ken, just to rest my eyes, Elizabeth said.

I will pull the bed out for you. Go get a comforter, Elizabeth.

Ken pulled out the bed. Elizabeth laid down on the sofa bed, and Ken joined her.

What are you doing???

Elizabeth, I need you like I never needed a woman.

Ken grabbed Elizabeth and kissed her. Elizabeth did not resist.

God, I love you, Elizabeth. I now know you still have feelings for me.

Ken, we just can't! Think about Alice.

You and Alice can come with me. Ryan doesn't deserve you, not after Mindy. He is still with her, Elizabeth.

I know. Let's focus on Alice first, then us later.

Fine, as long as you give me a chance to make you happy, but please give me five minutes to hold you.

I can't, I want you too bad, Ken.

Elizabeth could not hold back and began to kiss Ken.

Okay, Ken, this is enough.

I will respect your wishes. I need to get up, Elizabeth; I don't think I can stop myself.

I love you, Ken.

Ken's pulse raced.

I am going for a walk, Elizabeth; you rest.

Thank you, Ken.

Ken went for a walk; all he could think about was Elizabeth. He loved her deeply. He would have her. Ryan did not deserve her.

Elizabeth could not sleep. Ryan called and said Sister Mary had regained consciousness, but they were keeping her overnight and she needed x-rays. He said he would be home in two hours.

Elizabeth did not feel guilty about Ken. Ken came back in fifteen minutes and ran to Elizabeth. Elizabeth held Ken. Ken put Elizabeth on the kitchen table. He removed her dress.

Please, Ken!

Look me in the eye and tell me you don't want this.

I can't!

No condoms anymore, you will be the mother of our child.

I can't stop these feelings anymore.

Ken entered Elizabeth.

What have we done? said Elizabeth.

Nothing we both could have stopped.

We must wait now till I have left Ryan.

I will wait forever for you, Elizabeth.

God, what if my mother came upstairs, or the Fathers came down?

I'm sorry; I could not stop.

Eileen was awake; she came up the stairs and heard the whole thing.

Elizabeth, we need to talk.

I thought you were asleep.

I want to talk to my daughter in private, Ken.

Yes, Eileen.

Ken went downstairs.

I heard the whole thing, Elizabeth.

Before you say anything, I am in love with Ken.

You're still married!

That never stopped Ryan. I don't care if you are mad – it is my life!

I am not mad at you, bubble, just be careful.

I will Mother.

Ken, you can come upstairs now.

Ken was waiting on the stairs; he was afraid Eileen would tell Elizabeth to stop loving him.

Ken, take care of my daughter's heart.

I will, Eileen.

Then you have my blessing, but please tell Ryan it's over, Elizabeth.

I will, Mother.

WELL THE FIREWORKS WERE GOING ON DOWNSTAIRS. FUCKING THE DOCTOR'S WIFE ON THE KITCHEN TABLE. WHAT A SHOW.

Ryan came into the house.

Anything happen when I was gone?

Elizabeth blushed.

What's the matter, Lizzy?

Eileen left the room.

Ken?

Elizabeth needs to tell you.

What did you do, Ken?

Nothing you haven't done with Mindy, Ryan.

Elizabeth, you didn't!

Ryan slapped Elizabeth's face.

You fucking cocksucker! Ken punched Ryan in the face.

Ryan hit the floor.

If you ever touch her again I will give you the beating of your life!

Ken helped Ryan off the floor.

Lizzy, I'm so sorry, but I'm so hurt.

I'm sorry I hurt you, Ryan, but you hurt me so bad with Mindy. I want a divorce!

You're going to break up this family, Ken?

You already did that successfully, Ryan.

Elizabeth, are you alright?

I'm fine, Ken.

Ryan left the house.

Elizabeth, let's go check on Alice.

Okay, Ken.

They entered Alice's room.

ADULTERY IS A SIN, BITCH.

Ken, is that what you've done?

Yes, Father Seamus.

We cannot cleanse this house with adultery going on.

I'm not sorry, Father; I love this woman. It won't be a sin for too long, within a year she will be my wife.

I am leaving Ryan; one day I will tell the story, Father Seamus.

Okay, Elizabeth.

Thank you, Father Seamus.

How is she?

The same, Elizabeth. Don't give up on Alice, Elizabeth.

I never would.

LEAVE, YOU WHORE.

Shut up!

Elizabeth, the demon wants that reaction.

We will leave, said Ken.

That's a good idea, Ken.

I feel so exposed, Ken, but I don't regret it. I am too in love with you to regret it.

I love you very much, Elizabeth. Let's just be happy, Elizabeth.

We will, Ken; you never spoke of marriage, Ken.

You left me the first time; I never thought you would leave Ryan.

Neither did I; of course I wanted to marry you.

I wanted you to leave Ryan first. I have waited so long.

Me too, Ken.

Ken kissed Elizabeth's cheek.

You two have made your decision?

Yes, Eileen, I don't regret it! I am not guilty for loving Elizabeth.

No, you're not guilty in my eyes. Keep care of my daughter, heart. Always.

Ryan came back at night; he was polluted.

Ryan, you're drunk; what do you want?

I want a piece of you!

Go for it, Ryan!

Stop, please stop, you two!

Ryan don't even try me.

Ryan backed down.

Fuck you two, rot in hell.

Ryan went upstairs and passed out.

Now he knows what it feels like to be cheated on.

He never cared before; Mindy was very good about telling Ryan I was with you.

I know, but it didn't stop him from seeing her.

I don't care, Ken; this is what I want.

I will make you happy, Elizabeth.

I know you will.

Eileen walked into the kitchen.

Whatever you two decide is your business. I won't be backing Ryan. He cheated on you and didn't care. That does not go well with me. If he hadn't started this cheating, it never would have happened.

Thank you, Eileen; I will never betray Elizabeth.

WELL, THE LOVERS HAVE BEEN EXPOSED, THEY LIKE EVIL.

Give me a name, demon; God will not let you win.

MY FATHER WON LAST TIME, WHAT MAKES YOU THINK HE CAN'T WIN AGAIN?

Because I will banish you and every demon that comes, in the name of my Father.

HE IS A FAKE HERO; LUCIFER USUALLY WINS SOULS OVER, AND NOTHING WILL CHANGE THAT.

People who believe in the Lord will never fall.

WE WILL SEE, YOU ROTTEN MAGGOT. HOW'S THE BITCH DOING!

God will make you pay for that! Who are you, cruel demon?

I AM A DEVOTED DISCIPLE; I WILL NEVER LEAVE THIS CHILD, NOR WILL MY FATHER.

We need a break, Father Robert; let's rest.

Yes, Seamus.

I think it's time we both talked to Elizabeth and Ken.

Father Seamus and Father Robert went to deal with the commotion downstairs. Ken looked like he was ready for a fight as soon as Father Robert and Father Seamus entered the kitchen.

Ken, Elizabeth, is there anything we can say to change your feelings for one another?

No!

Okay, Ken, but you're not helping the situation.

I would do anything for Alice, but stop loving her mother is not one of them.

Okay, Ken, I will let you two decide what's best.

Please, some coffee, Elizabeth.

I will get you the coffee, Father Seamus.

Thank you, Eileen.

Eileen opened the cupboard and was swarmed by flies.

Lord of the flies!

The demon has revealed himself.

I should have known, I was swarmed by flies in my rectory.

Father Seamus and Father Robert went upstairs. They tried to open Alice's door, but it would not open.

Ken, we need your help!

Ken ran up the stairs.

What is it, Father Seamus? Alice's door won't open.

Stand back!

Ken kicked the door in.

Ryan woke up. *What's going on, Ken?*

Everyone entered Alice's room. She was covered in flies.

Holy Water, Robert!

Beelzebub, depart from this child.

A swarm of flies gathered around Alice.

What in God's name is happening to my child, Father Seamus?

Silence, Ryan!

In the name of Christ depart, Beelzebub!

Alice was lifted by the flies to the ceiling. Everyone looked in awe.

I said depart from this child, Beelzebub.

I AM SECOND IN COMMAND TO MY FATHER; I WILL NOT RELEASE HER.

You will depart, demon.

I DON'T THINK YOU KNOW WHO YOU'RE DEALING WITH! I AM LUCIFER, CHOSEN ONE.

Release the girl.

The closet door blew open. A horned beast emerged from the closet.

Good God, Father Seamus!

YOU AGAIN, THIS IS THE LAST EXORCISM YOU WILL PERFORM.

Alice lowered from the ceiling and was grabbed by the beast.

Downstairs the front door opened slowly. A monk walked through the door. Ken ran downstairs to see who had come through the door; Ryan followed.

Who are you?

I have come at Christ's command; step aside please.

The monk walked up to and into Alice's room.

Father Seamus looked to see who had come into the room.

My God, it can't be, said Father Seamus.

Lucifer, depart from God's child.

223

Lucifer and the demon shrieked.

I was sent to send you two back to hell! No demon shall ever touch this child again.

The swarm of flies descended into the floor. The horned beast ran into the wall and disappeared.

It is finished!

Father Seamus bowed down at the monk, and began to cry.

No need for tears, Father Seamus, please rise.

Padre Pio!

Yes, Father Seamus.

How can this be!

All things are possible for the faithful.

Padre Pio walked down the stairs and disappeared out the door.

Father Robert asked, *Who was that?*

Besides Christ, that was the greatest Exorcist to walk the earth: Padre Pio. You are truly blessed!

Alice gasped for breath.

Daddy? Daddy?

Yes, Alice, I'm here.

Help me!

I'm here for you, Alice.

Ryan picked Alice up and carried her to the living room couch.

Do you remember anything?

I only remember a pressure to my head, then it went black.

You truly have been called by God; remember that always.

Alice wanted to take a shower.

Please, everybody leave me for a while; I want to be on my own.

Why? asked Elizabeth.

To take this all in, and to have a hot shower.

We will leave you alone then, said Ryan.

Thank you, Daddy.

CHAPTER SIXTEEN

THE EPIPHANY

Sister Mary came home from the hospital.

Alice had a very long shower, and tried to think about the experience. As hard as she tried, she could not recall the last couple of days. Then a blinding white light went through her head, and she was filled with joy. She saw a man she believed was a monk.

Alice, you will walk a very fine line between good and evil; watch your step.

Alice knew these were the most important words ever spoken to her. Alice gave herself plenty of time on her own. Finally she could talk to the others and went down to the kitchen.

Sister Mary, does the calling of God come to you in a flash?

Mine did, Alice; I was three when I knew.

When can I start learning how to become a nun?

You will know.

How can I thank you?

Keep your commitment to God.

I will always.

The family seemed peaceful to Elizabeth. She knew she could not stay with Ryan; she was in love with Ken.

You are safe now, Alice. I need some time on my own now.

Why, Dad?

I need to be on my own for a while. Figure something out for my life, just as you just needed time on your own.

Alice was unhappy about the decision, but understood.

Okay, Dad, take as much time as you need.

Can I have a word with you, Lizzy?

Elizabeth and Ryan went up to their room.

Is there anything I can say, Lizzy?

I'm sorry, Ryan, no.

Okay, let me pack some of my clothes.

Where will you go?

To the Sheraton. It has a workout facility. A Christmas present to my family.

We will always be a family, just not together.

I know, Lizzy, you have a right to be happy. Ken makes you happy. I noticed all your extra pills.

Some of my pain was happening because of my emotions.

Probably, I did not help you. I will always regret that!

We have two different roads to go down, Ryan, but being a big part of Alice's life will never change.

I will never be able to pay you back, no matter what I do, Fathers, Sister. Also you, Eileen, and yes, you, Ken.

Thank you, Ryan, said Ken, *however much time you need, take it. I will be here for Alice.*

Take care of Eileen, and Elizabeth too.
I will.

Ryan kissed Alice and Elizabeth. He knew that would be the last kiss he would ever give his Lizzy. Ryan left.

I know it's a bit early, but will all of you stay and put up the Christmas tree?

Alice, I have a tape of the Exorcism; we need to get it to the Archdiocese.

This is all taped?
The important parts, yes.
I think that is very important, Father Seamus.
Let's get out the tree, guys.

The Fathers and Sister Mary left for the Archdiocese. The Archbishop did not need to see Sister Mary. Sister Mary thought women were valuable, that nuns and women needed to be heard from. She felt that a nun was a very important asset for an Exorcism.

Ken, come help me get the tree.
Of course, Elizabeth.
I can help too?
No, Alice, please try to relax, we'll get the tree.
Okay, Mom.

Ken and Elizabeth went to get the tree. In a box of Christmas ornaments Ken found mistletoe. He held it over Elizabeth's head.

A kiss, Elizabeth?
Yes, of course.

Ken and Elizabeth embraced.

Elizabeth found the star for the Christmas tree.
I think we'll buy an angel; it only seems right, Ken.
Do you think Alice can go to the mall?

She needs to see Delilah first, Ken.

Then let's get ready.

Alice, let's go see Delilah.

Sure, Mom.

Alice, Elizabeth, and Ken went to the Shipleys' house.

Delilah felt a pull towards the living room window. She saw Ken's Escape and was ecstatic.

Mom, Dad, Ken's Escape is outside in the driveway.

Delilah, don't get too excited; it may not be good news.

Dad, I see Alice!

Thank the Lord, said Shirley.

Delilah ran out to the driveway.

Alice! Alice!

Yeah, you little shit!

I'm so sorry.

I know!

We both have suffered from that board.

Sorry, I should not swear, it's not right for a future nun.

A nun?

Yes, Delilah, I have been touched by God, we both have. Come shopping with us.

Sure, I feel very much in the Christmas groove.

I think I will write a book, a way to pay back God.

I will have to find a way to repay God as well.

Please do, Delilah.

Everyone went to the mall. Delilah was worried; she now had bad feelings about the mall.

You guys, I don't know if I can handle the mall.

Why, Delilah? asked Alice.

I made some big mistakes here.

What mistakes?

I actually bought my own engagement ring at Max's.

Delilah, let it go, that's the best way to get past your experience.

I'll try, Ken.

They bought an angel first.

I want to buy everyone a nice present for Christmas, Mom?

I will get you a thousand out of the bank machine, Alice.

Thanks, Mom.

Don't forget the Fathers and Sister Mary.

Never! Delilah, stay with my mom and Ken, I'm going to Max's. I want to pick up those Christmas angels for the Fathers and Sister Mary.

Alice, I am not going to let Linda and Ivan wreck my favorite store for me.

That's the way to heal, Delilah.

You're the expert, Ken.

Everyone went to Max's.

Ryan was at Max's with Mindy. Elizabeth walked up to them.

You need time out for yourself, Ryan?

I'm pregnant, said Mindy.

If Mindy is pregnant, you'll need to be there for her, Ryan.

Thank you, Lizzy.

I want happiness for you two, Ryan.

Thank you, Lizzy.

Dad, I'm not happy with this.

It's the right thing to do, Alice.

She broke up my family!

It will just be an extended family, Alice.

I don't want you to be alone. Mindy, just make my Dad happy.

I will, Alice.

Alice and the others left the store and returned to the O'Doyle house.

Well, I guess you will have a little brother or a sister, Alice.

I guess that's not so bad.

Can I have a word with your mom in private, Alice?

Sure, Ken.

What's up, Ken?

Have you ever thought of having another child, Elizabeth?

Is that what you want, Ken?

Yes, Elizabeth.

Then let's start trying, Ken.

Thank you, Elizabeth.

Let's wait until I conceive before telling Alice.

Of course, Elizabeth.

I can't believe all my dreams are coming true.

I will give you a good life, Elizabeth.

I know you will, Ken.

Alice entered the room.

What's up, you guys?

Nothing, just future plans Ken and I have for our new family.

Delilah, let's go up to my room.

Okay, Alice.

Delilah and Alice went to Alice's room.

I can't believe it, Alice, we're both happy again.

Feels good, Delilah.

Alice, I'm very tired; can I lay down for a while?

Sure, I'll let you sleep.

Alice, what are you doing down here?

Delilah's tired, Mom; I'm going to let her sleep for a while.

Alice, are you really alright about Dad and Mindy?

Yeah, Mom, I don't want Dad to be alone. I think it's great about the baby.

You're excited?

Yeah, I am, and I heard you and Ken talking about having a baby.

Did you?

Yeah, I think it's great. I will get to live with a baby brother or sister.

I am so happy, Alice, about your mother and me having a baby.

I know, Ken, we'll have a big family.

You want that, baby?

Yeah.

Nobody noticed Delilah in the doorway.

Oh Delilah, you're awake. Delilah? Delilah?

Delilah Doesn't Live Here Anymore.

CPSIA information can be obtained at www.ICGtesting.com
Printed in the USA
LVOW06s1913221215

467457LV00022B/423/P